Little Sam Mountain

The Journey

Charles C. Fletcher

Published By
Fletcher Books
2310 Harris Circle NW
Cleveland, TN 37311

Little Sam Mountain — The Journey
Copyright © 2012 by Charles C. Fletcher.

All rights reserved. No part of this book may be reproduced, stored in a retrieval system or transmitted in any form or by any means without the prior written permission of the publishers, except by a reviewer who may quote brief passages in a review to be printed in newspaper, magazine or journal.

The names used in this book are the inventions of the author who apologizes should he have inadvertently used the name of any actual person. No event or incident in the story is intended to relate to or represent any actual incident.

ISBN: 978-1-4675-2703-3
Published by Fletcher Books
2310 Harris Circle NW
Cleveland, TN, 37311

Printed in the United States of America

Contents

A Talk With Mom 1
Leaving Home 11
Day No. 2 25
Sergeant Davis 33
Fort Bragg 43
Country Cooking 51
Letter Back Home 59
Travel Plans 63
The Airplane Ride 69
Back In England 85
Worcester 113
Journey Home 131
Sad News 143
Back Home 149
Sarah 159
Afterword 167

ACKNOWLEDGMENTS

The author wishes to thank his son, Gary Fletcher, for editing the typescript of *Little Sam Mountain — The Journey*. The Reverend Bruce Cayton provided the photograph for the book cover.

Little Sam Mountain

The Journey

A Talk With Mom

John was getting over the shock of losing Sarah Smith as his wife. He had long talks with his mother when his Dad and the others of the family were not home. For a few days after the shocking news about Sarah, John had many plans about what he would do with his life. Many times while growing up on Little Sam Mountain he had gone to his Dad for advice when he wanted answers to a problem. This time it would be his Mom he would depend on for answers.

"Mom, I was born and spent all of my life on Little Sam until I went into the Army, and I have never asked anyone why we lived up there on the mountain or who Little Sam Mountain belonged to and who built the log house we lived in," John said.

"It's sort of a long story, but I think we have time for me to tell it to you," John's Mom said.

It all began after me and your Dad were married. Like most newly married couples back when we were married, it was the custom for the husband to provide a house for his wife and himself. This was not easy to do in the 1930s. Money was scarce and, in our case, our families didn't own any land. They had started the same way we had to start: To find a place where the owner of the land would let someone build a house on their property in return for promising to help keep the fences repaired.

"That's how we ended up on Little Sam Mountain. Your Dad and his brother married two sisters, me and my younger sister. None of us had a house to live in at first. Your Dad and his brother began asking around to see who owned the mountain they had looked at and found a good place to build on. It had a good flat field with water on it. They found the owner, and they agreed to help mend his fences in return for their cutting down trees and building their houses. They built two log houses side by side: ours and my sister's house. Me and my family lived in our house until you left for the War, and then we moved off the mountain down into town in Canton. My sister and her family also moved when we left. Those two log cabins on Little Sam Mountain were our homes for a long time."

"Who owns Little Sam?" John asked his Mom.

"Here is the story as it was told to me," his Mom began. "A long time ago there was only one Sam Mountain. It was owned by a man called Sam Robinson. He had homesteaded the mountain and the pastureland around it. He had a son who was named Sam Robinson, Junior. He was about twenty-one years old when he married, and he built his house in one section of the pasture field across the wagon road going over the mountain to a place called Crabtree.

"After the younger Sam's marriage, his pappy told him he could have the entire mountain on the north side of the Crabtree road as a wedding gift. So, Sam Junior's part came to be called 'Little Sam Mountain', and the other part of the mountain came to be called 'Big Sam Mountain'. That was the way Little Sam Mountain got its name," John's Mom concluded.

"Where does the young Sam Robinson live now?" John asked his Mom.

"He lives in that big white house on the left of the road just where it starts up the mountain. You must have noticed the cider mill out in his yard. He has the only cider mill I ever saw around here. Everyone who has apple trees brings his apples to him to get them pressed into juice for cider and vinegar."

"I'm going over to see him tomorrow morning," John said.

All of a sudden, John seemed to be in better spirits and over the disappointment he had since returning from the War. The talks he had with his Mom seemed to get his mind on what he would do for his future.

Early the next morning after he had finished his breakfast, John told his Mom that he was going over to visit Sam Robinson, Junior. His Mom didn't question him about his sudden interest in the owner of Little Sam Mountain. She knew he would tell her about it sooner or later in the long talks they had every day.

John didn't have any trouble finding the Robinson house, and when he walked up the path toward it, he met Mr. Robinson feeding his chickens. He seemed to be enjoying feeding the chickens.

"Good morning," John said.

"Howdy, young feller. What's got you up so early today?" Mr. Robinson replied.

As John got closer to where Sam Robinson was feeding his chickens, Sam quit scattering the feed and took a good look at John.

"I believe I've seen you before," he said to John. "Didn't you sell me an old hen a few years ago?"

"I sold a man a hen a long time ago, but I never paid any attention to who it was I sold it to," John said.

"That was you, and you held me up on the cost. Charged me seventy-five cents for a fifty-cent hen. I never lost any sleep about it, though. She was the best laying chicken I ever had. She give me an egg every day until she died," Sam declared.

"But, I don't think you come all the way down that mountain to talk about chickens. What's on your mind?"

"I don't live up on Little Sam any more. When I went into the Army, my family all moved down into town. I only got back from the Amy about two weeks ago," John said.

John told Sam Robinson, Junior, that he had plans for building a house on the side of Little Sam and getting married. He didn't mention anything about Sarah.

"I was wondering if you would sell me a few acres of land over on the front side of the mountain. I picked out a place before I left. I laid some rocks on the corners of the part I would like to buy from you," John told Mr. Robinson.

Sam hesitated for a few minutes, pulled a plug of apple tobacco out of his pocket, took his knife and cut off a big chew. After a few chews and emptying his mouth of tobacco juice, he said to John, "Well, seeing that I don't have any cattle on the mountain, and I've not been doing any farming since I had my sixtieth birthday, I guess I wouldn't miss a little piece of that mountain. Must be over two hundred acres up there besides the fifty here at my house. I'm not doing anything right now, so what do you say we walk up there and have a look at the place you want."

"I'm ready to go any time you want. The exercise will be good for us both," John said.

On the way up the road toward Crabtree Gap, John and Sam stopped all along the way to rest. Sam said he wasn't used to walking over the mountains like he was when he was young. They called the trail leading up to the Gap a road, but it was somewhere between a sled road and a trail. When they were at Crabtree Gap, they turned right on a walking trail along the side of Little Sam. They soon come to a grassy field where John had marked out where he would like to build his house before he went off to the War.

"Here is one of the rocks I put down to mark off where I would like to buy. The other marker is a little farther over across the field. I want to buy all the way to the woods and down to that big rock cliff," John pointed and told Sam.

"From here I can see all the way to the city of Canton. There is the paper mill to the left. Sure is a big town. Must be at least twenty or more businesses there, and over there is the moving-picture theater."

"This sure is a pretty place to have a house," Sam said.

"Well, I would guess there must be about ten acres of land here that you want. I would have to have five hundred dollars for it. That would be fifty dollars an acre," Sam told John.

"That sounds a little steep, but I guess I'll take it. I have some money I saved during the War," John said.

"I'll pay for the surveying and get you a deed, and then you can pay me for everything at once," Sam told John.

Sam held out his hand, and he and John shook hands. This was the way deals were made binding in the mountains of Western North Carolina.

Sam and John had a lot easier trip off the mountain than the one up. They were soon at the Sam Robinson house, and John was about to head back to Canton when he said, "I don't know just when

I'll build, but when I do, I plan to have me some chickens, and I'll get the best layer in the bunch and give it to you."

"I bet you'll have to build a chicken lot that's fox-proof. There must be a lot of fox up there. Them fox hunters are up in that section about every weekend. Good luck with your chickens," Sam told John with a big grin on his face.

John also had a big smile on his face because he was happy about buying a part of the mountain where he and his family grew up. He walked as fast as he could on his way back to his Mom's house. He wanted to tell her the good news about buying a part of that mountain. It had long been a dream of his to someday be a landowner.

When John arrived at his Mom's house, all of the family were there. The first thing he told them was that he now owned a part of Little Sam Mountain. Not the old place where they used to live, but closer to the Crabtree Road.

"From where I will build my house someday when I find me a wife you can see the town of Canton and all the way to the top of Cold Mountain," John told his family.

No one mentioned what had happened when he had made the same plans when he and Sarah talked about it over three years ago. They were hurt as much as John by Sarah's not waiting to marry him.

"How much money do you have in the bank?" his Mom asked him.

"A little over fifteen hundred dollars, counting my mustering out pay," John said. "Mr. Robinson will have all of the papers ready this Friday, so I'll have to draw out five hundred dollars to pay him for the land. He thinks there is about ten acres, but from where I had the four sides marked, I bet there is at least fifteen acres," John said.

On Friday evening John met Mr. Robinson at his house on the Crabtree Road. Mr. Robinson gave John the deed for the land, and John handed him the money.

"I would feel better if you would count your money. Everyone can make mistakes," John said.

Sam counted his money, held out his hand, and shook John's hand. The land sale was final. The deal was bonded with a handshake.

On Sunday after dinner John asked the family if they would like to go see his new-bought mountain land. They all went up the mountain and John pointed out his land to them. The surveyors had little red flags on the sides that belonged to John.

"Sure is a pretty view from up here," John's mother said. All of the rest of the family agreed.

"Can I build me a house up here when I get married?" John's oldest sister Betty asked.

"I'll think about it," John said.

Monday morning after his Dad and the others were gone, John's mother asked John what plans he had for his future.

"Will you get a job at the paper mill where your Dad works, or work somewhere on a farm?" she asked.

"Been thinking about traveling around for a while until I decide what I want to do. May look around for a wife," John said as he grinned at his mother.

"Quit teasing me," John's mother said as she slapped him on his shoulder.

Leaving Home

"Guess I'd better get busy packing a few clothes if I plan on searching for my fortune out there. Don't really know where I'm going or how long I'll be gone," John said to his mother.

"Kind of sad to see you going off again, but you are a grown-up man and know how to take care of yourself. I hope you find the answer to what you are looking for and come back home. Sure would like to see you build that house up on Little Sam Mountain. That's where you belong. How are you going to travel?" his mother asked.

"Guess I'll start off riding the bus to Asheville and then start hitch-hiking. Thumbing a ride is pretty popular since all the soldiers started home. I'll wear my uniform, and that pretty much guarantees me a ride if someone comes by and has room for one more passenger," John told his mother.

"Where are you going first after you leave Asheville?" his mother asked.

"Thinking about working myself over toward Fort Bragg. Pretty sure there will be some of the old career soldiers still there," John said.

John told his family he would be leaving the next morning and that he would send letters all along and let them know where he was and what he was doing.

"Always planned to come back here after the War and settle down in these mountains where I was raised, but I've changed my mind," John told his family.

Next morning John was up when his Mom was cooking breakfast. He recalled that he and his Mom had a similar talk the morning he left for the Army over three years ago. His Mom gave him the same advice that she gave him before about always holding his head up high and making her proud that he was her son.

"Always be a leader, don't follow others," she said.

John waited until all the family were off to work and school before giving his mother a big hug and telling her he was on his way. Once again John was going off not knowing what his future would be or where his journey would take him.

John didn't use his duffel bag to carry his belongings in. He had bought a backpack. This was all he needed for what he wanted to take along on his journey.

Another goodbye to his Mom, his pack on his back, and he headed to the bus station on the street near the movie house.

"When will the bus be leaving for Asheville?" John asked the man at the ticket counter.

He looked at the clock and said, "Be another thirty minutes if he is on time."

The bus was on time, and John was on his way to the big city of Asheville. John would not start hitch-hiking until he was out of town. Someone had told him that the city had some kind of law against bumming in the city which included trying to hitch a ride. John would have to walk to the other end of the tunnel where the road ran through the mountain. They called the tunnel Beau Catcher Tunnel. John wondered why they named the tunnel "beau catcher".

John didn't have to wait long after he came out of the tunnel to get a ride. A car pulled to the side of the road, and John trotted over to where it had stopped.

The driver was all dressed up in a suit and was wearing a necktie. He opened the door and asked John, "Where are you headed, Soldier?"

"Going down to Fort Bragg, but was planning on stopping at Kings Mountain. Met someone in England that I would like to visit before going back to the Army camp," John told the driver.

"Going over to Charlotte, but I'll be going through Kings Mountain. Get in. Be glad to have some company. I'm on the road a lot with my sales business and sort of get lonesome riding all alone. How long have you been in the Army, Sergeant?"

"I'm not in the Army just now but may join back after I talk with them at Fort Bragg. I've only been out of the Army for about three months.

"I spent over four years all together. Started at Fort Bragg, went to England for a couple of months, and sailed over to North Africa to help the English fight the Germans. Then moved over into Italy and fought my way over to France and Germany.

"That's why I want to stop at Kings Mountain. I was wounded in Europe and was sent back to a hospital in England. I meet someone there while getting the bullets taken out of me. That's when the War ended and I got to come back home," John told the salesman.

"Wow! Didn't' know I had a war hero for my passenger," the driver said to John.

John blushed a little and told the man who had picked him up that he was not a hero.

"Only did my job like thousands and maybe over a million other boys did. Lots of them mountain boys out there came from them mountains in North Carolina helping fight them Germans and the other people over the other side of the ocean," John said.

As they rode across the twisting road over Chimney Rock Mountain, the driver asked John question after question about his experiences in the War. John would only answer general things about the Army and didn't give any details about the shooting and stuff. He wanted to forget all about those things. He didn't want to talk about seeing his buddies die as they fought that war.

After they were nearing Spindale, John's driver said to him, "What do you say we stop here in Spindale and have a sandwich? Been a long time since I eat breakfast,"

John had brought enough money with him for eating and a place to sleep while he was traveling but was planning to only spend as little as needed.

"You're the driver. Stop any time you like. I'm not too hungry but will have a cup of coffee," John said.

The salesman didn't say anything to John as he pulled in the parking lot at a restaurant near town.

"Here we are. Come on in. Never like to eat alone. I like to have someone set with me when I'm on the road," he said to John.

The waitress led them to a table and handed them a menu. On that menu the first thing he saw was "Hotdogs — Ten Cents — With All the Trimmings — Ketchup Free". He was trapped. Hungry or not, he could never turn down a hotdog. After all, only in North Carolina could he find them. Especially with real meat dressing on them.

John waited for his driver to order his lunch, and the waiter asked John what he wanted.

"Not too hungry, but I will have one of them hot dogs and an orange drink. And bring the ketchup with it," John said.

"That looks so good, I think I'll try one," the salesman said to the waiter.

"Bet you will like it," John said.

When John finished eating he asked to be excused. He was going to the restroom. He locked the door to the restroom and pulled up his shirt. Around his waist he had a money belt. The one he had worn while in the Army. He unzipped the belt and took out a dollar. This was to pay for his hot dog and drink.

When he got back to the table, he asked the waiter how much he owed him.

"Not a thing," the waiter told John. "Your friend paid for both of the meals."

They were leaving, and John thanked the salesman for the hot dog.

"Didn't mean for you to buy that for me. I have money to pay," John said.

The car pulled out, and they were on their way again when the salesman said to John, "My name is Bob Johnson. I work for a factory over in Tennessee that manufactures stoves. They make gas stoves as well as coal and wood burners. My job is to sell them, and I travel a lot. Especially here in North Carolina. I come to Charlotte about every week."

"Sure see a lot of cotton mills since we left the restaurant," John said.

"The closer you get to Charlotte, the more cotton mills you'll see. Especially around Gastonia. Only a couple around Kings Mountain though," Bob told John.

John saw a sign along the road that said, "Kings Mountain — Two Miles". He straightened up where he was slouching in his seat and tucked his shirt in. He was a little fidgety not knowing where he would start looking for the little nurse he had met in England in the hospital. "Maybe she was still in the Army and didn't come back to Kings Mountain," John was thinking to himself.

"Kings Mountain is not a big place. You holler when you want off," Bob said.

"Guess somewhere near the hospital would be fine," John told Bob.

"You not sick are you?" Bob asked John.

"No. Just thought this would be a good place to start looking for my friend," John said.

Bob pulled the car over to the curb and pointed to a building across the street.

"There you are, Soldier. That's the hospital over there," Bob said to John.

John got out, thanked Bob for the ride, and held out his hand. "Glad to have met you. Thanks for the ride and the hotdog," John said.

Bob left John standing on the sidewalk looking toward the hospital wondering where he should start his search for June Henson, the nurse he met in England.

"I guess the most likely place to look for a nurse would be where someone was sick, and that would be the hospital," John said to himself.

John went to the desk that had a sign on the front that read, "INFORMATION". He waited his turn and asked the lady if there was a nurse in the hospital by the name of June Henson.

"Does she work here?" the lady asked.

"I don't know. The last time I saw her or talked with her was in a hospital in England," John told her.

The information receptionist ran her finger over the name "Henson" and wrote some telephone numbers down. She handed the list to John and pointed to a telephone on the wall near her desk.

"You're welcome to call these names and see if you can locate the person you are looking for," she said to John.

John began to call the Henson numbers and asking if they knew a June Henson who was a nurse in the Army. The first three numbers didn't know her, but the fourth number he called told him that she was their daughter.

"Can I speak with June?" John asked the lady who had answered the phone.

"I'm sorry but June is not here. She is in the Army over in England," June's Mother told John.

John told June's Mother who he was and that he was passing through and wanted to visit her.

"I would love to have you come to our house and talk with me and June's Dad," Mrs. Henson told John. "If you would tell me where you are, my husband will come pick you up, and you can visit us."

"I'll be standing in front of the hospital. I'm wearing my Army uniform, so it shouldn't be hard to find me," John told her.

John didn't have to wait but about ten minutes until a big black car pulled up to the hospital where he was waiting for Mr. Henson.

He walked over to the car and said to the driver, "I'm John Dowdy, a friend of your daughter June."

"Get in. My wife is waiting for you. Don't be surprised if she asks you a million questions about our daughter June," he said to John.

Jane's Mother and Dad lived on the edge of town in a big two-story, white house. When John went in the house, June's Mother was waiting for him and her husband.

"My name is Sally Henson, and this is my husband George, if he hasn't already introduced himself to you," June's Mother said to John.

John followed Mrs. Henson and her husband into what he guessed was called the living room. He was hardly seated before Mrs. Henson began asking questions about June. Before he could answer a question, she would ask another one. She finally stopped asking long enough for John to tell her what he knew about her daughter June.

He told about getting wounded and how he first met June in the hospital in England. He told about the surgery by Dr. Stone to remove the metal from his legs and hips. He also talked about his future plans after getting out of the service after the War was over.

"Did June say anything about getting married once she was back home?" Mrs. Henson asked John.

"She mentioned that she had a boyfriend in Kings Mountain but never mentioned anything about getting married," John told her.

"I'd better go and find a hotel before dark," John said.

"No need for you to sleep in a hotel when we have two extra rooms here. You can spend the night with us,' Mrs. Henson said.

"Do you have any children besides June?" John asked.

"We have one son and June. They were our only children. Sam, our son, lives in Gastonia. He works as purchasing agent for a cotton mill there in Gastonia. They wouldn't let Sam in the Army. He has a limp from an injury from playing football in high school. We should have taken him to Duke or somewhere beside the hospital here. They may have helped him. Don't know if he will ever get married. Said he didn't have time for a girlfriend. Too busy with his job," Mrs. Henson told John.

Mr. Henson finally got to talk with John.

"That cotton mill you saw when you come into town is where I work. I am the plant Manager. Been with them for over twenty-five years. The boyfriend that June mentioned works there, also. His father owns the mill. He takes care of their money. Sort of like an accountant," Mr. Henson told John.

"Are you sure I won't be a bother sleeping here tonight?" John asked.

"Not one bit. Be glad to have you," Mrs. Henson said.

"I have to get up early tomorrow and attend a meeting over in Charlotte. That's on your way to Fort Bragg, and you can ride over there with me if you want to," Mr. Henson told John.

"That would be great. Give me an early start, and if I'm lucky hitching a long ride I'll be at the camp before night," John told Mr. Henson.

"If you can be ready around seven, we'll leave and stop at the all-night diner just outside town and get some coffee and doughnuts," he said to John.

"I'll be ready. Where is the room you want me to sleep in?" John asked

Mrs. Henson led John to a room upstairs and showed him where the bathroom was and extra covers for the bed if he needed more.

John shut the door and stood there for a few minutes looking the room over. He could see that this was their son's room when he was growing up. There were pictures and trophies on the wall that he had from his football, basketball, and other things he had done. John had to envy their son a little bit because he had never had the opportunity to go to school and do any of these things.

After a quick bath, John was in bed. His first day on his adventure was a tiring one. Especially answering all the questions from the people he met that day.

Day No. 2

John didn't have any trouble falling asleep because his first day on the road was a tiring one. He was awake and dressed when Mr. Henson pecked on his door.

"Ready to go any time you are," he said to John.

John opened the bedroom door before Mr. Henson could go back down the stairs, his backpack on his shoulder and ready to leave.

As they left the house they were very quiet so they wouldn't wake Mrs. Henson.

When they arrived at the all-night diner, John and Mr. Henson had to go all the way near the back to get a table. The place was filling up fast with employees from the cotton mills. They were in a hurry to eat breakfast before they went to work.

"Pretty good food here. I've eaten breakfast here several times, and they are always crowded," Mr. Henson said to John.

"Hope they can find us way back here. I'm kind of hungry," John said.

A young girl came to their table with a pad and pencil in her hand.

"What will you have, Handsome?" the waitress asked John.

John blushed and told Mr. Henson to order first.

"I'll Have two eggs, over light, sausage, toast, and a cup of coffee," Mr. Henson told the waitress.

"I'll have the same, only cook my eggs done," John said.

"Got it. Be back in a jiffy," she told them.

"I haven't decided if I will re-enlist in the Army or not. Probably make up my mind after a visit at Fort Bragg. Kind of want to go back to England and visit, also. If I do go to England, I'll be sure and visit Jane and tell her about my visit with you," John said to Mr. Henson.

The waitress brought their food and handed each of them a check.

"You can pay up front on your way out," the waitress told them.

John was on his second day of the trip to Fort Bragg and hadn't spent a nickel of the money he brought with him. Mr. Henson picked up his check and paid for his breakfast.

"No need for you to do that. I have money and should be paying for your breakfast" John told Mr. Henson.

"Better save all the money you can. It's a long way to England, and you will need it," he told John.

John was soon on his way toward Charlotte and another try for hitch-hiking a ride.

"I'll drive you out to Highway 74 and let you off at a little place out of town. Good place to catch the traffic where they will be going toward Fort Bragg," he said to John.

Mr. Henson pulled his car over on the side of the road and said to John, "Good luck. Hope you make the Fort before dark. Would be good if some trucker picked you up. They're usually on long trips."

John didn't have to wait long until a big truck pulled over to the side of the highway. He hurried to the side of the truck and the driver told him to get in.

The driver pulled the truck back on the highway and asked, "Where are you headed, Soldier?"

"Down to Fort Bragg. How far are you going?" John asked the driver.

"This is your lucky day. It just so happens that I am headed to the Fort also. Got a load of clothes to deliver to them," he told John.

"My name is John Dowdy. I'm from Canton. Just got out of the Army a little while back. Started at Fort Bragg then moved to England for a couple of months. They shipped me to North Africa to help the English soldiers. After the War started, I moved all the way through Italy and nearly up to Berlin in Germany. Got shot and had to move to the hospital in England. Now I'm thinking I may re-enlist," John told the truck driver.

"Looks like you've moved around quite a bit," he said to John.

"My name is Eddy Russell. All the people who know me just call me 'Big Ed'," he said to John.

"Thanks for giving me a ride. Especially all the way to the Fort," John said to Big Ed.

Big Ed must have been lonely traveling all over the country alone except when he picked up someone hitching a ride. This was one of those times when he was asking John questions faster than John could answer him. John didn't mind and was thankful he was getting a ride all the way to Fort Bragg.

It also seemed that truckers liked to eat, and they knew where the best food was. About noontime Big Ed pulled his truck over to a truck stop along with about another dozen truckers.

"It's 'bout time for something to eat," Big Ed said. "You hungry, Soldier?"

"Been a long time since I eat breakfast, and I could eat a little something. Don't know if I'll be back to Bragg before the Mess Hall closes for supper," John said to Big Ed.

Big Ed parked the truck and told John to be careful when he got out of the truck.

"It's a pretty long step down there,"

"I've never rode on a truck as big as this one. Been on the Army six-by-sixes lots of times, though," John said to Big Ed.

The dining room was as crowded as the parking lot at the truck stop. John had never been in a restaurant where all the customers were dressed so differently and the drivers had their favorite caps or hats that they never bothered to take off when they were eating. Also some of them had long hair and beards. There were no two of them who looked like they were from the same family. John couldn't keep from staring at them.

They found a seat, and the waiter was there to take their order as soon as they sat down.

"What are you gentlemen eating?" the waiter asked John and Ed as he handed them the menu.

"Think I'll have beef stew, mashed taters, turnip greens, and some hot peppers on the side. Better bring me some of that apple cobbler with a scoop of ice cream on it," Big Ed told the waiter.

"How about you, Soldier?" the waiter asked John.

"Got any hotdogs?" John asked.

"Sure do," the waiter told John.

"I'll have two dogs with all the trimming, a big orange drink, and bring the catsup," John said.

"Any desert?" the waiter asked John.

"Some apple cobbler would be fine," John said.

"Thought you were hungry," Big Ed said to John.

"Not as hungry as you are. Where are you going to put all that food?" John asked Ed.

The waiter brought the checks along with their food and laid them beside each of their meals. Big Ed reached over and picked up John's ticket and put it in his pocket along with his own.

"Give me the checks. I want to pay for your lunch, not you to pay for mine," John said to Big Ed.

"Save your money, Soldier. The company I drive for pays me well and I can afford it. You soldiers don't get paid enough," Big Ed told John.

John didn't argue with Ed. This was his second day of his travel and he hadn't spent any of his money he had in his money belt under his shirt.

The traveler and his truck driver friend were soon back on the road headed toward Fort Bragg. Big Ed kept the speed right on the limit where he wouldn't get a ticket from one of the patrolmen who hid behind the billboards all along Highway 74.

John was reading the road markers to see if they were getting close to Fort Bragg when he saw a sign that said, "Fayetteville — Next Exit".

Big Ed also saw the sign and said to John, "We'll be on the Fort in another thirty minutes,"

John was a little excited and also a little nervous thinking about trying to locate someone he knew when he was in Basic Training.

Big Ed pulled his truck up to the guard station, stopped the motor and got out. He handed some papers to the MP who looked at them and told Big Ed to take a left on Robert Street and go to the warehouse on the end of the street.

John had got out of the truck and was standing there at the check station. He walked over to the MP and asked him where he could find a sergeant by the name of Brad Davis.

"You mean old Sergeant Davis who's in charge of the Guest House? You can find him over on Fifth and Ed Streets. He is always there. Never goes out," the MP said to John.

"Are you a guest?" the MP asked John.

"Sort of. I just got out of the Army a few months ago. Sergeant Davis was my platoon sergeant during Basic Training," John told the MP.

"Get in the truck, and I will drop you off. Five Army blocks is a pretty long walk," Ed said to John.

"If that is not the sergeant you are looking for, flag me down when I come back, and I'll take you back to Charlotte," Big Ed told John.

Sergeant Davis

Big Ed stopped his truck and said to John, "Good luck, Soldier. Enjoyed having you along for the trip."

After Big Ed left, John stood on the curb and had a good look at the buildings to see if he recognized them. Everything looked different because he had never been in this section of Fort Bragg. There was a large sign on the front of one building that said, "GUEST QUARTERS".

"This must be it John said to himself."

He walked up the sidewalk leading to the front of the building where the sign was. When he opened the door, there sat a sergeant at the desk who he hadn't seen for over three years, but he recognized him immediately.

"Sergeant Davis," John said.

"John Dowdy!" Sergeant Davis hollered to John.

The Sergeant started to stand up, but instead fell back into his chair. John could see that something was wrong with his good friend, Sergeant Davis.

"Had a little accident since I last saw you. I have a little trouble with my legs," Sergeant Davis said to John.

"I was shot in my legs while in France, but after the doctor removed the bullets, I can walk real good," John said.

"I had a car accident," Sergeant Davis said.

"When did that happen?" John asked.

"Do you remember the day I borrowed the Captain's command car and took you to the bus station over in Fayetteville when you were shipping out to Fort Benning for infantry training?" the Sergeant asked John.

"Yes. You took my best buddy Wolf and me to catch the bus," John said.

"After you two got on the bus, I went down to a beer joint called 'The Town Pump' for a short drink. After I left to come back to Bragg is when I had the car wreck," Sergeant Davis told John.

"Guess I should tell you all of the story and get it off my mind," the Sergeant said. "Oh, by the way, did you and that girl you always talked about get married after you came back from the War?" Davis asked John.

"No. Things didn't work out as we had planned. She was married when I got back home," John told Sergeant Davis.

"Let's go across the street to the PX and get a bite to eat, and when we get back, I'll tell you the whole story of my life," Sergeant Davis said to John.

Davis picked up a walker that he used when walking with his crippled legs and led the way toward the door down the hall from the office where he was when John arrived.

"Only a little way to the PX, and I get around pretty well with this thing that they gave me after I got out of the hospital. Had lots of practice walking after over three years," Sergeant Davis said to John.

While they were eating their lunch, John noticed a sign on the front of the door that said, "Help Wanted". He asked Sergeant Davis what kind of help they were looking for.

"People who work here in the PX. Working on the counter selling, in the dining room waiting on tables, and that kind of stuff," he told John.

"I need a job. Do you think they would hire me?" John asked Sergeant Davis.

Sergeant Davis motioned to a soldier standing behind the counter where they sold cigarettes and tobacco. He walked over to where John and Sergeant Davis were sitting and said, "Hi Sarge. How're things going with you?"

"Fine. Just fine. Legs getting better every day," Sarge said.

"John, this is Corporal Bill Coven. He is the Manager of the PX," the Sergeant said to John.

"This is John Dowdy, a good friend of mine who was in my platoon back before the War. He needs a job. Do you think you could use him?" the Sergeant asked the Corporal.

"Sure could. When can you start to work?" the Corporal asked John.

"I could start on Monday if that would be OK. I want to visit the Sergeant a couple of days. Haven't seen him in over three years," John told Corporal Coven.

"That will be fine. I'll bring you the application papers, and you can fill them out and bring them back tomorrow when you come back to eat. I'm sure you will be back, because Old Sergeant Davis eats most all his meals here," the Corporal said to John.

Sergeant Davis and John finished eating their lunch and went to the check-out counter in the front of the PX. John handed his check and money to the soldier at the check-out, but Sergeant Davis pushed John's money back and told John that this lunch was on him. John had got another free meal since he had left on his journey. The only money he had spent so far was for the bus ticket from Canton to Asheville.

After the two old buddies got back to Sergeant Davis's office, John asked the Sergeant what was his job was.

"I am in charge of making sure that visitors and traveling soldiers who need lodging have a place to sleep. Got this job after my accident," he told John.

"The story I'm going to tell you is a part of my life that no other person on this earth ever knew about. I'll tell you because you are the only person I have ever trusted to keep a secret," Sergeant Davis told John.

"When I first met you at Fort Bragg as a new rookie in this Army I was a phony. I was pretending to be the perfect soldier in this Army when I was the worst example at Fort Bragg. I was an alcoholic. I had to drink every day to keep going on as a leader.

"It all started after my last visit back home. Do you remember me telling you that I came from just outside Knoxville, Tennessee? A little town called Oak Ridge. That's where I grew up as a child.

"While I was in high school I fell in love with the prettiest girl in school. Sort of puppy love at first, but after we finished school and I volunteered for the Army, we considered ourselves as serious lovers. Or at least I did. I took leave every chance I had and caught the bus to Oak Ridge. I asked her to marry me, and she said yes. She was to name the date for the wedding and tell me the next time I came home.

"I was the happiest soldier in the Army and working as hard as I could trying for a promotion that would mean more money for us to set up our first home. On my next trip back home, I asked her what date she had decided on for the wedding. She said, 'I'll tell you on your next trip back home.' I had a strange feeling that she was stalling on setting a date but didn't say anything to her.

"I always wrote her about when I would be coming home, but for some reason I decided to surprise her on one visit. I got a seven-day furlough and caught the bus for Oak Ridge. Had to change buses in Charlotte and Asheville and arrived at the bus station in Oak Ridge a little after six o'clock in the evening. I didn't bother to go home. I went straight to Fanny's house. She wasn't home, and her Mom said she was at a friend's house just across the street. Fanny's Mom gave me the house number, and I walked over to her friend's house and knocked on the front door.

"When the door was opened, I saw not only Fanny but a soldier with her. She was speechless for a moment but finally said to me, 'Brad, this is Captain Jack Henderson, my future husband. He is stationed at Oak Ridge where I've worked since you went in the Army. We've been dating for a long time, and I should have told you instead of my keeping you thinking I would marry you someday,' Fanny told me.

"I was speechless. I didn't say anything to them. I turned and walked away. I didn't go to my home there in Oak Ridge. I went back to the bus station and bought a ticket back to Fort Bragg. While I was waiting for the bus to arrive, I asked a taxi driver where I could buy some moonshine. I didn't have to go anywhere. The taxi driver also sold liquor. I bought a bottle and began drinking before I got on the bus back to Asheville. That was the beginning of me becoming an alcoholic.

"I never was sober until a few weeks after I met you and your soldier buddy, Wolf. Fanny had destroyed all of my dreams, and I was trying to forget what she had done to me. I would drink all night after working with the recruits every day. I had myself programmed to do what I was teaching them.

"When my Mom died, I went back to Oak Ridge for her funeral. I didn't see Fanny, but someone told me that the Captain she married divorced her about six months after they were married and shipped overseas somewhere. She was asking if I ever came back to visit. I never went back to Oak Ridge again. I had no reason to visit after Mom died. I did have a sister and one brother but never heard from them. None of the family seemed to care what I was doing.

"After you were assigned to my platoon, I began to take notice of how happy you and Private Wolf were and how you went out of your way to help the other soldiers and me in my outfit. It wasn't easy, but I began to turn my life around. Instead of locking myself in my room and drinking until I would pass out, I began to be a part of what the soldiers did every time they were not on duty. I joined in what they did to unwind after a hard day's training to become a soldier. You, John, were an example of all the happiness I was missing.

"I never drank another drop of whiskey until the little drink I had with Captain Pugh the day he told you and Wolf that you were transferring to Fort Benning to take infantry training. That one little sip was the beginning of staying away from my drinking. The day I took you and Wolf to the bus station was another sad day in my life. After you left, I went to a bar and tried to forget losing such a good friend like you.

"Instead of going back to camp like I should have done, I drank most of the evening. I somehow got the Captain's command car started and on the road. Then it happened. I passed out, and the car ran out of the road and turned over. When it stopped, I was under it. I don't remember anything that happened until I woke up with both my legs in casts.

"Well John, that's the story of my life and where I am today. It all started the day Fanny destroyed my dream of a long happy life with her." Sergeant Davis smiled at John as if he was relieved of a burden.

"I know how you felt. Let's forget the past and try for a better life in the future," John said to his Army buddy. "I've got to find me a place to sleep tonight."

"No need to look any farther. What I do best since I took this job is to provide a place away from home for those who are visitors at Fort Bragg. You are a visitor, and I just so happen to have a vacant room. Just sign your name on this book, and

I'll show you what you can consider your new home as long as I am in charge of this Guest House," Sergeant Davis told John.

Fort Bragg

John's job at the PX started on Monday morning. Corporal Bill Coven, who was in charge of the PX, told John that he would be working at the tobacco counter.

"Never smoked or chewed tobacco, but I'm sure I can find what kind they want when they ask for something," John told the Corporal.

"If you have any trouble, just call me and I'll give you a hand," Corporal Coven told John.

John didn't have any trouble, and the tobacco counter was the easiest job in the PX. He watched as the other employees went about their assigned jobs. He noticed that the section that sold beer and wine was the busiest place in the PX.

Sergeant Davis came over to eat lunch with John about twelve o'clock.

"The food is not too bad here, but I like to go over to the main Mess Hall for a meal every now and then. They have a much larger selection of food. Even have seafood every Friday evening," the Sergeant said to John.

Sergeant Davis had someone take his place at the reception desk at five every evening and on Saturdays and Sundays. During those times he and John caught up on what took place since John left for Fort Benning down in Georgia.

After dinner one evening, Sergeant Davis asked John to come to his room so they could talk. His room was larger than the room John was given. There were special things for the Sergeant to hold on when he was moving around in the room and bathroom. The room was equipped just for him.

"How did you get to stay in the Army after you injured your legs?" John asked his friend.

"You remember Captain Pugh who was the company commander when you were here? Not only was he my boss; we were very good friends. He was the one who loaned me his car the day I had the wreck. After the accident, I was to be discharged from the Army when I left the hospital. Captain Pugh came to see me. I asked if there was any way that I could stay on for a few more years so I could finish my twenty years in the Army. He went to the General who was in command at the Fort and asked if it would be possible to keep me on. The

General told Captain Pugh if he could find a place for me he would let me stay until I got my twenty years in. Here I am: the boss over the Guest House at Fort Bragg," the Sergeant told John.

"Good to have friends," John said.

"Where is Captain Pugh now?" John asked Sergeant Davis.

"About a year after I had the accident Captain Pugh, shipped out. The last I heard from him he was headed for the Pacific War with the Japanese," Davis told John.

"Sure glad I didn't have to go over there in them jungles. Heard that there are lots of jungles and snakes everywhere. I'm as scared of a snake as I am the Boogeyman," John said.

John and the Sergeant asked each other questions until nearly midnight. Sergeant Davis even told John what a good soldier Zimmerman made in spite of his love for baseball.

"Zimmerman went on to OCS and received his commission as an officer. Last I heard he was a top-notch leader," the Sergeant said to John.

John and Sergeant Davis usually ate their meals together, but sometimes he had to eat alone at the lunch counter in the PX. This was one of those days when he usually sat alone. Today was the first time anyone asked to sit with him. And this was the first time a girl asked to eat lunch with him. He was a little nervous because he had never sat with women-folk other than with his sisters, his Mom, and the two girls at the fish-and-chips place in England when recovering from his injuries at the hospital.

"My name is Jerry," the girl said to John. "I'm sure you have seen me at the souvenir counter here in the PX. I wanted to get acquainted with you before now, but that Sergeant is at your table most every time you are.

"He is my best friend here at the Fort," John told Jerry.

"I've been working here for over a year now, ever since my husband went overseas. He should have been back, but for some reason he likes it over in France. That's where he is stationed. I get awful lonely staying here day and night all alone and was wondering if you wanted to go out to town for a movie or something?" Jerry asked John.

John was really nervous after Jerry invited him out for a date, and what really shook him up was that she was married to a soldier. He couldn't finish eating his lunch. Somehow he had lost his appetite. John pushed his lunch back and got up from the table.

"I've got to get back to work now. Glad to have met you," John said to Jerry.

John managed to pretend that he was busy. He had the feeling that that woman Jerry had an eye on him. He was nervous and maybe a little bit scared of her.

John didn't mention Jerry to the Sergeant when they were eating supper, but as soon as they were home he told him what took place while he was eating lunch that day.

"Better stay away from that woman," Davis said to John. "She is a flirt and troublemaker from day one. Don't blame her husband for transferring overseas to get away from her. Wouldn't surprise me if he never comes back."

"Do you think I could find a job somewhere away from the counter up front near where that woman works?" John asked Davis.

"Don't think so unless you want to work in the kitchen with Tubby the Chef," the Sergeant said.

"May look the kitchen over and have a talk with Tubby tomorrow when I have a break," John said.

"The Chef's name is Mono Lucas. He came from Greece with his family to the States when he was only a baby. Seems that cooking comes natural to Greek people. He volunteered for the Army just before the War ended. Got the name 'Tubby' because he is sort of short and chubby. Must be from sampling the food he cooks here for the PX dining room," Davis told John.

"Greeks must be born cooks. The best dot dog I ever eat was from the Greek restaurant where I grew up in Canton. Don't know where he learned to make hot dogs because they cook a lot of spicy food like the Italians do over in Italy," John said to Sergeant Davis.

The next day John went into the kitchen during Chef Lucas's break after breakfast. He was determined to get away from that woman Jerry who seemed to be looking at him all day at the tobacco counter where he worked. He hadn't been comfortable since she joined him for lunch and tried to get a date with him.

"My name is John Dowdy. I work here in the PX but would like to work somewhere besides on the tobacco counter. Do you have any openings here in your kitchen?" John asked the Chef.

"Are you serious? I always have openings here. No one likes the kitchen. The only help I get is from the rookies who are put on KP," the Chef said to John.

"I'm serious. I would like to work here if you can find something I can do," John said to the Chef.

"Can you cook?" the Chef asked John.

"I helped my Mom cook a lot when I lived up on Little Sam Mountain, but we didn't have all them fancy groceries you cook here. I helped cook squirrel dumplings and gravy, crackling corn bread, saw-mill gravy, roast ground hog with candied sweet taters, and stuff like that," John told the Greek Chef.

"Never cooked any of those meals, but they sound good. Where can I buy supplies like that?" Chef Lucas asked John.

"Don't know around here, but you could use other things and cook the same way, and they would never know the difference if you called it them things," John said to the Chef.

"You're hired. When can you start to work?" Lucas asked John.

"Have to talk with Corporal Coven before I can say. Wouldn't just walk off 'less he had someone to take my place," John told the Chef.

When John told Sergeant Davis about the job in the kitchen helping Chef Lucas cook, Davis asked John if he was sure he wanted to get up at five in the morning and work in that hot kitchen. John told him he wouldn't mind waking up early. Told Davis he did this when he was home before the Army.

"I did the milking and fed the animals every morning while Mom was cooking breakfast. This gave me an early start when I went squirrel hunting. Had to find a good place before the squirrels woke up," John said to Davis.

"You wouldn't be asking for the job with Lucas just to get away from that woman in the PX would you?" the Sergeant asked John.

"Could be. But the cooking pays more money, and I need to save a little so I can go visit in England," John answered Davis.

"OK. We'll tell Corporal Coven first thing tomorrow morning," Sergeant Davis told John.

"I'll put the sign 'Help Wanted' up again. Hard to keep help here," Corporal Coven said to Sergeant Davis and John.

"I'll go tell Chef Lucas that I'll be ready to start working with him at five o'clock tomorrow morning," John told the Sergeant and the Corporal.

Country Cooking

Getting up and ready to be at the kitchen in the dining section of the PX wasn't easy since John had been sleeping late while living at the guest quarters with Sergeant Davis. When he arrived in the kitchen, Chef Lucas was already giving orders to the other people working for him.

When the Chef saw John, he wiped his hands on the apron he was wearing and said, "Glad to have you helping me do the cooking. For a taste of that cooking you helped your Mom cook on whatever you called that mountain, how about some of them cat-head biscuits and saw-mill gravy as a starter for breakfast?"

"I'll need some flour, buttermilk, sweet milk, baking powder and lard," John told the Chef.

"Got everything but the buttermilk and lard. Never seen any lard. What does it look like?" Chef Lucas asked John.

"Guess I can make out without the buttermilk, but I have to have some lard. I saw a bucket of it setting on the table when I was in here yesterday," John told the Chef.

John walked over to a big wooden table and pointed to the gallon bucket. "Here is the lard," John said to Lucas.

"Oh, that's called shortening. Never heard it called lard," he told John.

"We made our own lard up on Little Sam Mountain. Melted all the fat from the hogs we killed and let the grease get sort of thick and stored it away to use for frying and baking," John said to the Chef.

"How many people will be here for breakfast?" John asked.

"Usually around twenty-five show up for breakfast. Have a few more for lunch," Lucas told John.

Guess I better bake about fifty cat-head biscuits and two gallons of saw-mill gravy. Nobody can get by 'til lunch on one biscuit," John said.

Chef Lucas went in the supply room and brought the supplies John asked for and laid them on the big wooden table.

"Over there on the wall are pots and pans. You get the ones you need. There is the oven for baking the biscuits," Lucas said to John.

"Need a little vinegar," John said to the Chef.

Chef Lucas scratched his head and asked John what he needed the vinegar for.

"Use a little in some of the milk for my sour milk, seeing that I don't have any buttermilk," John told his boss.

The Greek Chef was watching John as he was working like a beaver mixing and stirring the flour and other ingredients together for the cat-heads. He soon had the first pan ready for the oven and was patting and rolling out another batch for the oven. He then started on the saw-mill gravy by using some of the shortening and flour to scorch in the big frying pan. The Greek Chef couldn't keep his eyes off what John was doing. Wasn't long before John had a mountain of biscuits as big as his fist and about two gallons of brown-milk gravy.

"Made fifty of these and plenty of gravy to go on 'em." John said.

The other cook in the kitchen had fried eggs and sausage along with some oats for the breakfast customers. Everything was what they usually had for breakfast, except John's biscuits and gravy took the place of the usual toast.

When the first ones came for breakfast and went through the chow-line, they were given the usual breakfast that they were used to getting every morning — eggs, sausage, oatmeal, and coffee. When they saw the biscuits and gravy, they asked where their usual toast was.

"Got something special this morning. Do you want one or two of these cat-heads?" John asked.

"I'll only have one. Never seen anything like that," the diner said to John.

John put a biscuit on the table, broke it in half and covered it with the thick brown gravy. He repeated this until everyone was at their table and eating. John saw one of the first ones who went through the line coming back to the food line.

"Can I have another of that thing with the gravy on it?" he asked John.

"Sure can. Cooked enough so all of you can have two if you want 'em. They are mighty fine with some honey or molasses on them instead of the gravy," John told them.

John saw a big smile on Chef Lucas's face when he saw that the first meal from his new helper was a success. He had never had anyone come back for seconds with what he fed them for breakfast.

"What do you have planned for the lunch meal?" Lucas asked John.

"All depends what you have in the supply room," John said.

"Go in and see what you have that you can cook that will be different from what I cook every day," Lucas said to John.

John found him a pencil and paper and went in the room that was cooled for the meats and things that needed to be kept in a cool place. He wrote down the meats and cheeses then went into the other supply room. He looked around and made him a list of what he wanted that was not there.

"You have about everything I need except buttermilk, canned apples, and a variety of spices. How long will it take you to get these things?" John asked his Chef.

"I'll send someone over to the Warehouse and should have these things back by nine o'clock," Chef Lucas said.

John wrote a list of what he planned to cook for lunch to add with what was usually on the menu. He listed the following: squirrel dumplings, turnip greens, and black eye peas. He handed the list to Chef Lucas.

"Where are you getting squirrels to make dumplings with?" the Chef asked John.

"I've seen a lot of squirrels around camp but would be afraid to get a gun and go out shooting them like I did back home on Little Sam. They would put me in the stockade if I went around killing these tame squirrels. I'll cut up some chickens, add a little flavor, and they'll never know the difference," John told Lucas.

Only the people from the mountains knew the names of what John cooked. Any substitution in the food was never noticed, and to them it tasted like whatever John named the food.

Word soon spread about the new food at the Mess Hall for the PX. Chef Lucas and John couldn't cook enough for them. The soldiers were coming from the main Mess Hall instead of eating in their assigned areas. By the end of the week the officers were coming for some of this strange food. There was no way for Chef Lucas and John to feed them all.

"I'm going over to my Captain and ask him for some help in getting everyone to eat where they should be eating. Not all of them here with me," Chef Lucas said to John.

"How about sending your new helper over to the Officers' Mess to cook for us," the company commander said to Lucas.

"Sure don't want to let him go, but I'll ask him. He's not in the Army. Was here for his Basic but was in the War and wounded somewhere over in France or Germany," Chef Lucas told his Captain.

Lucas told John about them wanting to have him for their cook. John told Chef Lucas that the only way he would move and cook for the officers was that they also transferred him. And if they did send him to the Officers' Mess, he should get a promotion.

"I'll go tell the Captain, but don't think he'll go along with promoting me," Lucas said to John.

When the Chef told his Captain what John said, he didn't say anything for a couple of minutes.

"Well, looks like that cook John drives a hard bargain. I'll have to go talk with the Major and get back to you," the Captain said.

The following Monday, Chef Lucas and John were in the Officers' Mess Hall cooking breakfast. The Chef was promoted up one rank, and John was given a raise in pay.

It wasn't long until the officers' dining room was too small to seat the regular diners. Officers were coming to eat from other companies.

The General who was commander over all of Fort Bragg was soon asking for everyone to eat at their own companies. After the General talked with several company commanders and ate a few meals at the Officers' Mess where Lucas and John were cooking, he decided that they should be his special cooks.

That ended the war of the cooking services of Master Sergeant Mono Lucas and his assistant cook, John Dowdy.

LETTER BACK HOME

January 15, 1945

Dear Mom,

    I should have wrote to you and the family before now, but have been awful busy since I left Canton.
    I rode the bus to Asheville then hitched a ride with a salesman over the Chimney Rock Mountain to Kings Mountain. I visited the Mom and Dad of the nurse I met in England at the hospital after I was wounded. I spent the night with them, and Mr. Henson gave me a ride to Charlotte. George Henson, June's Dad, was Manager of a cotton mill in Kings Mountain.
    My next ride was with a truck driver named Eddy Russell. He went by the name of Big Ed. He was on his way to Fort Bragg, so I was lucky. I didn't have to

hitchhike anymore that day. Big Ed took me to where Sergeant Davis lived on the Fort. Guess you remember me telling you about him being my boss all through Basic Training when I first got to Fort Bragg.

The Sergeant is all crippled in his legs. I won't tell you about what happened until I come back home. Sort of sad, but glad to see him again. Beside Bill Wolf, I guess Sergeant Davis is the best friend I ever had. You remember Bill Wolf, the Indian boy that went in the Army when I did. He was from somewhere around Maggie Valley.

I have to get up real early like I did at home since I started the cooking job here at the PX Mess Hall. I first worked in the PX but didn't like that, so I got this job with the Head Chef. He goes by the name "Tubby". His real name is Mono Lucas. Come over here from Greece when he was a baby. We work pretty good together. He knows how to cook all the good stuff we eat on Little Sam. He had never heard how to cook country eating until I showed him. Everybody likes this kind of food now that they have tasted it.

I'm saving my money so when I get back home I can build my house up on Little Sam. You know, on the piece of land I bought from Sam Robinson. May be another year before I see you and the rest of the family.

Bet my brother Joe and sisters are all grown up now. Does Betty still talk about going to school to be a nurse?

Is Dad still working in the paper mill? Tell him I said hi and to take care of himself.

May have missed some of the news from around here, but will write you again. I'll try not to wait this long next time.

Tell everybody "hi" for me, and you take care of everyone.

Your son,
John

P.S.: Didn't mention that I may go over to England to visit some of the people I met when I was there in the hospital. They talk sort of funny, but after a while I could understand what they were saying.

All their talk is sort of proper and fast. Not like the slow way we talk.

    That nurse that took care of me in the hospital didn't come back to marry the boy she was sort of engaged to. Don't think she wanted to marry him from what I gathered when I talked with her Mom. If I hear anything about her, I will let you know in my next letter.

    Bye for now.

Travel Plans

A year passed since John arrived at Fort Bragg to visit his good friend Sergeant Davis. Since he left his Mom's home, luck had been with him. The only money he had spent for his trip was the bus fare to Asheville from Canton. All his meals were given to him by those who gave him rides. After he met Sergeant Davis, his luck was again with him. He was given a free room at the Guest House that Sergeant Davis was in charge of. He didn't pay for his meals after he began the job as a cook with the Greek Chef, Lucas.

John was off from his cooking job every Saturday and Sunday. He and the Sergeant didn't leave the Guest House only long enough to eat their meals. All the other time was spent visiting with each other talking about the things that had passed in their long military life. Davis had many questions for John about all he saw and done during the War.

"Sarge, do you have any ideas how I can hitch a ride to England?" John asked his friend Davis.

"Seems like I remember a couple of majors who were with me here at the Guest House for a few days. If I remember correctly, they were sort of retired from full-time duty. Said they were hanging on to get their thirty years in. Both had been in WW II flying bombing missions over Germany. They mentioned that they were sort of like chauffeurs for the Army. When someone needed to take a long trip, they would fly them. Most of their flights were for the USO at Army stations in Europe. I'll do a little checking and find out if they are still around here," Sergeant Davis told John.

John and the Greek Chef were cooking the noon meal for the Mess Hall where the General ate most of his meals. John asked if he knew the officers that usually ate here.

Lucas said that he had become acquainted with a few of them.

"I'm looking for the Majors who are pilots who take special people where they need to fly," John said to Lucas.

Lucas pointed to where two officers were sitting at a table. They had finished eating and were drinking their coffee and talking. John went over to where the majors were sitting and introduced himself.

One of the majors said to John, "My name is Major Jackson, and this is Major Finley. You're the new cook here aren't you?"

"Yes. Been helping the Chef for the last few months. Major, are you the pilot who flies people around for special meetings and things?" John asked.

"Yep. Me and Major Finley changed our mission from flying bombs to hauling all sorts of passengers. Mostly people who still go over to Europe for shows with the USO. In fact, we have a trip over to England and Germany the first of next month," Major Jackson told John.

"Think you could give me a ride over to England on the next trip?" John asked the Majors.

"Would be glad to if you will wear your uniform. That would make you look like you were a part of the crew," Major Jackson told John.

"Good, I still have my uniform with me," John said.

"I'll see you later and give you more details on the time and where you can meet me," Major Jackson told John.

John was very excited about finding a free ride to England. He hurried up with his work in the kitchen and hurried home to tell Sergeant Davis the news.

"That's them. That's the two majors I was telling you about. They are two old pilots who are only marking time for the day they retire. Nothing GI with them. They pretty well do their job the way they like," Davis told John.

The next day Major Jackson motioned for John to come over to the table where he and Major Finley were eating lunch.

"We're leaving for England on Monday week about 0800. That will be next Monday," Major Jackson told John. "I have to make a stopover in Nashville, Tennessee to pick up a hillbilly band that is going to entertain at the USO in England and somewhere in Germany. Will you mind riding along with a bunch of guitar and fiddle players? Be best if you could be at the plane about 0700. I hope to be in the air by 0800."

"I'll be there," John said.

John told his Greek cooking buddy that this would be his last day helping him in the kitchen. He explained that he was leaving for England next Monday morning. John didn't tell Lucas how he was traveling overseas.

"Sure hate to see you leave me. I've learned a complete new way to cook since working with you. Guess I'll have to keep cooking country food and forget the Greek and Italian cooking,"
Lucas told John.

Sergeant Davis and John visited one more time before they would be parted again when he went to England. He didn't have much to pack for his trip. Only the clothes he had when he arrived.

"I need to deposit the money I have before I leave for England," John told Davis.

"You can use the bank here on base if you want to. That's where I have my account," Sergeant Davis told John.

"I'll do that the first thing tomorrow morning," John said.

"I'll need someone to give me a ride to the airbase over to Pope Field about 0700 next Monday," John said to his buddy Davis.

"I'll have one of the MPs take you over. Too far to walk. Must be at least three miles to the airport," Davis said to John.

On Friday John had all his business taken care of at the post bank and the clothes packed that he would take with him on Monday morning. He was excited about going but was sad that he was leaving his good buddy. It had been over a year since he came to Fort Bragg to visit his old Army Sergeant.

"Going to miss you" Sergeant Davis said to John.

"I'll miss you a lot, but I will be back to see you in a couple of months. Just wanted to see some of the friends I made while I was over there," John said to his good buddy.

After lunch on Sunday, John went by to say goodbye to Corporal Coven but made sure he didn't bump into that woman by the name of Jerry who worked in the PX. He then went to the Officers' Mess to speak with Sergeant Lucas before he left.

John didn't sleep well on the Sunday night before his trip to England. He was up and waiting for the MP to pick him up for the ride to the airfield. Sergeant Davis was also up early to see his best friend, John Dowdy, leaving him again.

At exactly 0630 the MP was at the Guest House where John had lived since coming back to Fort Bragg. Sergeant Davis and John gave each other a big hug and said goodbye.

"Be back in a few months," John said as he was getting in the jeep the MP was driving.

The Airplane Ride

John didn't speak to his driver until he said thank you when he got out at the airfield. This was all strange territory to him. He had never been around where there were airplanes every place he looked.

At 0730 Major Jackson and Major Finley met John where he was waiting for them.

"Exactly on time, Sergeant," Major Jackson said to John.

The two Majors kept walking toward a big airplane where several soldiers were checking it over from front to back. The four engines on the plane were idling, and smoke was coming out the back end of the engines.

When John and his pilots walked up the steps into the plane, John saw that there were four soldiers located at various locations.

"Looks like all our crew are here and ready to go," Jackson said to John and Major Finley.

Major Jackson said hi to his crew as he introduced them to John.

"Have you flown very much?" Major Jackson asked John.

"Never been in an airplane in my life. In fact, never seen many. Only the ones that flew over me when I was in the Army during the War," John told Major Jackson.

"Come on up front, and I'll tell you a little about our plane," the Major told John.

John followed Major Jackson up to the front of the plane. The two pilots sat side-by-side, and John took a seat in back of them. John's eyes were wide open and staring at all the gauges, numbers, and hands he saw in the front of the plane. He stretched his neck trying to see out of the window of the plane, but all he saw were the four big engines in the front with big propellers turning very slow.

"This is an old C-54 transport plane that was remodeled for flying special people where they need to go on a long trip. It's used mostly by the entertainers that go overseas to entertain the military people that are stationed there. This trip we'll be going to England, France, and Germany. The only cost for this entertainment for the troops is what it costs to take them and bring them back," Major Jackson explained to John.

John saw the propellers turning faster, and someone had closed the doors on the side of the plane. The noise from the engines began to get real loud and the plane began to move away from the buildings where they were sitting when John first arrived at the airfield.

"Getting ready to lift off," Major Jackson told John.

"We have a couple of stops before we get to England," the Major told John. Got to fly over to Nashville, Tennessee, and pick up a hillbilly band that plays on the Grand Ole Opry. I don't care for that kind of music, but other people like it."

"That's not too far from Little Sam Mountain over near Canton where I was born and raised," John told the Major.

"We fly over all the mountains on the way to Tennessee. If it's a clear day this morning, you can see all the mountains in the Smokies," the pilot told John.

The engines on the plane began to get louder, and the plane was acting like it was trying to move but couldn't. This all changed suddenly as the plane moved forward real fast and John was holding on to his seat although he had a seat belt on. When he did get where he could look out of the window, the buildings on the ground looked like little doll houses.

"Hang on, Soldier. We'll soon be high enough to clear the top of the Smoky Mountains," the pilot said to John.

"Hope I can see Little Sam Mountain when we cross the mountains in North Carolina," John told the pilot.

The noise that sounded like the plane was struggling had now changed to a steady hum, and they were now flying level instead of going in a steep climb. John was straining his eyes looking for the mountain that he grew up on. Every so often a big white cloud would block his view of the ground below the plane. When the plane was high enough to be over the mountains, all John could see was a smoky-like cover where the ground was not visible.

"Guess this is why people call them The 'Smoky' Mountains," John said to the pilot.

"Sorry you couldn't see the mountains as we went over, but this is usually the way it looks every day," the Major told John.

After they were over the mountains, John was enjoying his first plane ride. The smoky and cloudy skies were gone, and he could see the cars on the highway on the flat land. The fields that had crops planted in them looked like someone had painted a picture in them. Every field was a different color from the many different things that were growing there.

Soon the plane was coming lower to the ground, and John could see the airfield near Nashville where they would land. The plane John was on began to circle around and didn't land.

"Having to joy-ride for a few minutes until the plane on the ground takes off and gets out of my way," the Major said to John.

After a long ride around the airport, the plane that was on the ground went like it was going straight up and soon disappeared in the sky.

"Fasten your belts. We're going down," the pilot told the rest of his crew on the plane.

John was watching as the plane went down toward the runway. It looked like they were going straight into the ground, and John shut his eyes and didn't open them until he heard the tires make a squeaking sound when the plane was coming to a stop. At the end of the runway, the plane did a turn and slowly came to the airport building where several people were waiting.

The Major stopped the engines and lowered a ladder-like ramp to the ground so they could get off the plane.

"Better stretch your legs. Going to be a long time before you will be on the ground again," the Major told John.

The two Majors and John went over to meet five men that were wearing cowboy hats and cowboy shirts. They were all carrying some sort of musical instrument. A couple had guitars, one had a banjo, another had a fiddle, and the other one had a mandolin.

"You gentlemen must be the band that I'm flying over to Europe for the USO shows for the military people over there," the Major said to them.

"Yep. They told me that the soldiers over there like country music, so we volunteered to play a few shows for them," the tall one with the white cowboy hat said to the Major.

"My name is Josh Walker. We call my band 'The Tennessee Walkers'. I do most of the singing," Josh told the Majors and John.

"Better get loaded up while they are putting more fuel in the plane. This is our last stop until we stop up in Canada to refill for the six hour flight to England," the Major told the band leader.

"Oh, I also have a rule on my plane that no smoking will be allowed while we are in flight. Do any of you smoke?" the Major asked.

The shortest man, who had the banjo, raised his hand and said, "I love a smoke every now and then."

"Better get a good smoke now before we leave. If I catch anyone smoking on my plane I may strap a parachute on him and push him onto one of the small islands between Canada and England," the Major told the banjo player.

The band was soon on the plane along with their musical instruments. John found him a seat up front near where the two pilots sat for driving the plane. After the plane was filled with gasoline and the steps were put back inside, the door was closed. The four engines on the C-54 plane that was redesigned for flying passengers instead of equipment and soldiers was getting up to speed and began moving toward the runway away from the airport terminal.

"Get them seat belts on," the Major yelled out above the noise from the engines.

After taxiing the plane to the end of the long runway, the Major sped up the engines until the plane was like it was trying to break loose as if it was tied down. As soon as the brakes were released, the plane sprang forward so fast that John felt like he was pressed to the back of the seat and couldn't move his body. Once the plane was in the air, everything was back to normal. John could move in his seat again.

"Shore glad I was in the Army instead of the Air Force. I'm not complaining, but I like being on the ground a lot better than up here in the air flying around," John said to his friend, the Major flying the plane.

"Be over Canada in about three hours," the Major said to John.

"Reckon we'll see any Eskimos or polar bears?" John asked the Major.

"Don't think we will. Canada is a little too far south," the Major told John.

"Probably see a lot of snow and maybe some moose before we stop for more fuel," the Major said to John.

"You take over," the Major said to his co-pilot. "I'm going to check on our guests up front. Haven't heard any music or singing from them. Always thought that these hillbillies were great at singing sad songs about their women folks," the Major said to John with a grin on his face.

"How is everything going?" the Major said to the band leader, Josh Walker.

"Just fine," Josh said to the Major.

"Having a little problem keeping the banjo player from lightin' up a cigarette. I keep reminding him about what you told him would happen if he does," Josh said.

"I mean everything I said about smoking on my plane, and I will tell you why I feel this way," the Major told Josh.

The Major had all of the band to get closer to him so he could tell why he never had any smoking on the plane.

"Well, it was back during in the early part of 1944 while I was transporting soldiers over in England. Don't exactly know how many was on the plane when it happened. Most all the soldiers smoked, and I didn't care for them doing so. Well, I was approaching land when I saw smoke coming out of the front end of the plane. I asked the co-pilot to take over, and I went up front where all the commotion was and saw the flames from the fire. I began helping get the fire out with my bare hands. We got the fire out, but several soldiers were burned pretty bad. My hands were stinging, and when I looked at them I saw that my right hand was burned pretty bad. I hollered to the co-pilot to find a place to land and get down as soon as he could. The major who is at the controls now was that co-pilot," the Major told the band players.

"When we were on the ground, an ambulance was waiting, and three of the burned soldiers were taken to the hospital. All of them had very bad burns on their body. I had an MP to drive me to the hospital to take a look at my hand. The doctor and nurse covered the burned spots with some kind of grease and bandaged it up.

"'You are lucky,' the doctor told me. 'Take a couple of months, but could be fine except a few scars,'" the Major told them as he held his hand out so the musicians could see the scars from the burns.

"I was lucky. One of the soldiers died the next day, and the others had to have skin transplanted on their body," the Major told them.

"What caused the fire?" Josh asked the Major.

"Well, as I said, I didn't care for soldiers to smoke on the plane, but when one of the soldiers was lighting his cigarette, his lighter came apart and the fluid flew all over them and caught fire. Lucky the plane didn't burn with all of us inside," the Major told his audience.

"From that day on I warned everyone that was on the planes I would be the captain on, that there would never be any smoking on my plane," the Major told everyone.

"I have a pretty good feeling that you people will do as I have asked you to. That is, except the banjo player. I keep having the feeling that he wants to sneak and light up for a short smoke, and I am warning you all what will happen if any of you are caught smoking."

The Major then went back to the controls of his plane.

"We'll be in Newfoundland in about an hour to make a short stop for fuel before heading to England," the Major said to John.

Everything was quiet for the rest of the trip to Newfoundland and the stop to gas-up for the long, six hour trip to England. The hum of the engines was causing John to nod off and nearly go to sleep. He left his seat up near the cockpit of the plane and wandered out to the back of the plane. The band members were beginning to drop their heads and shut their eyes. Only the short banjo player was wide awake. He was restless and fidgety like he was having withdrawal from missing his smoking for so long. John could see that something was bothering him, so he began a conversation with him.

"Going to be a long time before we get back on the ground after the stop for gas," John said to the banjo player.

"Sure would like a smoke. Been near three hours since I had a cigarette," the short man said to John.

"If you don't think you can make it all the way to England, you'd better get off when they stop for gas. Sure would be bad if you tried to smoke and the Major found out. I believe he would really strap a parachute on you and push you off on some island out in the ocean," John said to him.

"Going down in about five minutes, fasten your belts," the Major announced to his passengers.

John fastened his belt and stretched his neck so he could see out the front of the plane. John was looking for a big city, but all he saw was a landing strip that looked like it was on an island. The only building near the airfield was small with a radio antenna on the top. Along side of the building John saw what he guessed to be the fuel truck.

"Canada being such a large country, I was expecting a large city with a big modern airfield," John said to his pilot.

"Newfoundland is a large island off the coast of Canada. About all there is here are a few small villages, a paper mill, and miles of trees," the Major said to John.

The plane was soon on the ground and stopped near the small house that served as the air terminal. When the steps were lowered to the ground, the banjo player was on the ground with a cigarette in his mouth puffing like a steam engine.

The Major came down to where the little man was standing and said to him, "You are really hooked on them things. If you don't think you can do without one for the next six hours, you had better get your banjo and other belongings and not go with us for the rest of the trip."

The Major went to where Josh, the band leader, was standing. He said something to him and went into the small air terminal. Josh went to where his banjo player was puffing away on his cigarette and said something to him. The short man threw his cigarette down, put his foot on it and returned to his place on the plane.

The fuel truck moved away, and all the people that were supposed to be on the plane were back in their seats. The Major motioned for Josh to come up where he was at the front of the plane.

"I noticed that your banjo player was the first one back in the plane. What did you say to him back there?" the Major asked Josh.

"I told him that he would not have another cigarette until we are on the ground in England even if I had to tie him to his seat," Josh told the pilot.

"Good for you," the Major said to Josh.

They were flying against the time, and daylight was soon turning to night. The time was five hours earlier than in the eastern part of North America.

John was straining his eyes in the window looking for ships or anything else he could find in the darkness above the dark ocean below them. He spotted a faint flicker of light at a distance. John asked the Major what he thought it could be.

"Could be a lighthouse on an island or a passing ship," the Major told John.

An hour had passed on the long trip to England, and the only noise was the hum from the engines of the plane. It seemed that all the band members and others on the plane had gone to sleep. Only John and the two Majors were wide awake.

"Take over for a few minutes," the pilot said to his co-pilot. "I want to check on our passengers."

When the Major was up front he saw that everyone was nodding and nearly asleep. Everyone but the short banjo picker, and he was sound asleep and snoring. Josh, the band leader, opened his eyes and straightened up in his seat.

"How is everything going?" the Major asked Josh.

"Fine. Just fine. Don't think Shorty will be wanting a smoke any time soon. I gave him a little something so he would get a little sleep. He probably won't wake up for another six hours," Josh said to the Major.

"Good. Glad you did. I was a little worried about him," the Major said to Josh.

The Major returned to his seat at the controls in front of the plane. John was beginning to drop his head like he was sleepy. He stopped trying to see anything in the darkness but did see a few stars scattered around the sky.

The darkness of the night passed fast, and the morning of the next day would come faster, for there was a five-hour difference between England and North America. The sun was rising in the east.

John had fallen asleep sitting in his seat and was awakened when the Major hollered.

"There she is. I see Scotland. Everyone better wake up and get your seat belts on. We'll stop and gas up for the rest of our trip," the Major told everyone.

Back In England

Shortly the plane was on the ground and stopped at the air terminal. Everyone was awake except Shorty, the banjo player. He was sleeping like a baby. Josh, the band leader, threw some cold water in Shorty's face. He jumped up, but the seat belt kept him in his seat.

"Wake up. Time to stretch our legs a little," Josh said to his banjo player.

The two Majors, John, and the five men in the band all were on the ground in front of the plane stretching their arms and legs. Everyone was watching Shorty to see how soon he would have a cigarette in his mouth, but he didn't look for one. Everyone was surprised but didn't dare mention this to him.

"Maybe he has quit smoking," the Major whispered to Josh.

The service man that had filled the plane with fuel gave the Major a snappy salute and said, "All ready to go, mate."

They were back in the air headed down the coast of England toward an airfield near the city of Worcester. This was near where the American hospitals and soldiers were that would be entertained by Josh Walker and his Tennessee Walkers at the hospitals and other USO shows in Europe.

John's luck was still with him. It so happened that one of the hospitals was where he was when he was wounded during the fighting to free Europe from Hitler and his Nazi government. He was hoping that the hospital he was in was still there and also that the little nurse from Kings Mountain, North Carolina, was still there. June Henson had been his nurse all the time he was in the hospital recovering from the wounds he got somewhere over in France or near Germany. He didn't know where he was when his squad was ambushed by the German soldiers. He had remarked to June that she reminded him of Sarah when he saw her in the hospital when he was recovering from his wounds.

"There is the airfield where we will be landing," the Major pointed out to John.

"Looks awful small. Like the one we landed at after the trip over the ocean," John said to the pilot.

"About as close as we could get to the hospital where Josh and his gang will be playing and singing," the Major said.

As the plane circled to approach the field where he would land, John pointed to the building with a big red cross on the top and said to the Major, "That looks like the building where I was after the War."

When the plane taxied up to the air terminal and the engines stopped, everyone gathered up what they wanted to take with them and got off the plane. The Major asked that everyone wait near the plane until he came back.

"They are bringing a bus to take us to the hotel in town," the Major told them when he returned from the office in the air terminal.

The bus came shortly, and when they were all on board, the Major said to them, "We have reservations at the hotel in a town called Worcester. We will be staying there until the USO show is over and then fly over to France. We can eat our meals there in the hotel."

"I will leave in the morning and try to find the hospital where my friend is stationed," John said.

"All the plans are made for the band's schedule while they are on this trip until I fly them back to Tennessee," the Major told them.

"Today is Tuesday. Tomorrow the bus will take all of the band to the hospital where they will visit the patients in the wards. Then on Thursday, Josh and his gang will put on a show for the soldiers stationed at the hospitals in the Malvern area," the Major announced to Josh and his team.

When the bus arrived at the hotel in town, they all went to the lobby of the hotel.

"Would you gents please sign the guest register?" the hotel clerk asked the Major and his group.

The two Majors were first to sign. The senior Major, the pilot, turned to John and said as he patted John's shoulder, "You're next Sergeant."

After they were all registered and rooms assigned, the hotel clerk said to the Major, "The dining room is on the second floor, and dinner will be served at five o'clock."

After everyone had gone to their rooms, cleaned up, and dressed, it was nearly six o'clock when they went into the dining room. All of the men that belonged to Josh's band had dressed in their clothes that they always wore when they were entertaining. The dining room was beginning to fill up fast with the guests staying at the hotel. When Josh and his group came in, all the guests turned and were staring at the dressed-up cowboys.

Major Jackson, Major Finley, and John were seated at the head table. All of Josh's men were at one long table. The Hotel Manager was standing at the door leading into the dining room where he was greeting his dining guests when he noticed that everyone had their eyes on Josh and his band.

"When will the music start?" one of the guests asked the Hotel Manager.

The Manager didn't answer. He went to the table where John and the Majors were seated and asked Major Jackson if he could have a word with him.

"Sure. What's on your mind?" Major Jackson asked.

"Could you and the leader of those cowboys speak with me in private?" the Manager asked the Major.

Major Jackson whispered to Josh, and the two of them followed the Manager into a room at the back of the dining room.

"The five cowboys have caused a lot of excitement here in the dining room. I was thinking if you would have a short concert, the meals for all of you tonight will be paid for by the hotel," the Manager suggested to the Major and Josh.

"What do you think?" Major Jackson asked Josh.

"Don't go anywhere. I'll be back in a jiffy," Josh said.

The jiffy was short, as Josh was back in a couple of seconds.

"It's a deal," Josh said. "It will take a few minutes to go get our instruments." And off Josh went with his buddies.

The Manager announced to all the diners that he had a treat for them. There would be a free concert by the famous Josh Walker and The Tennessee Walkers all the way from the "opera" in Nashville, Tennessee.

When Josh and the band entered the dining room, there was a standing ovation. Everyone was standing and clapping their hands, including the Majors and John.

The band played two popular country songs, and Josh sang a song. They set their guitars and other instruments in back of their tables and picked up their menus. They didn't look at the prices of the food because they would not have to pay for anything.

Josh said with grin, "Like Ol' Man Tucker, we sang for our supper."

The Hotel Manager was really pleased with the reception of the entertainment in his hotel. After the Major and his group finished their dinner, the Manager asked all of them to come into his office.

"If you will do the same show again tomorrow evening, all of your meals for the rest of your stay will be paid by my hotel," the Manager told them.

They all looked at each other, and Josh spoke up: "If the rest of you agree, we'll do the show for another night."

The Manager hurried out of the office and into the dining room.

"Ladies and gentlemen. I have a special announcement. Tomorrow evening there will be free entertainment for all guests in the dining room by Josh Walker and The Tennessee Walkers. They came all the way from Tennessee in the USA to entertain the military here in Europe."

The Manager had a big smile on his face when everyone stood and clapped their hands.

After breakfast the next morning, the group that came to visit the patients in the hospitals loaded into the bus for their ride to an area called Malvern. They wore their cowboy outfits but didn't bring their guitars and other musical instruments. John and the two Majors were going along with them. John was anxious to find the nurse that took care of him when he was a patient in the hospital.

The Majors went along to visit the patients and the doctors.

The doctors, nurses, and all the workers heard that the guests were coming, and they had the patients in their best hospital clothes. There was a greeting group waiting when the bus stopped at the first of the many buildings that covered the countryside.

John was the first to get off the bus and went straight to the reception committee.

"Would you happen to know what building that a nurse by the name of June Henson is in?" John asked a Captain in the group.

"Sure do. She is stationed in the third ward up the side of this hill," the Captain told John.

As John was walking up the hill, he recognized the trees and bench where he met Tony after he was sent to the hospital and Tony's arm was removed to save his life. He was in John's squad when they were ambushed by the Germans.

When John opened the ward door and went inside, he didn't see June. He went to the nurses' station and looked inside but there was no June Henson there. A nurse that John had never seen was sitting at a desk writing something on a pad of paper.

"Pardon me," John said to the nurse.

She raised her head and smiled when she saw John.

"Can I help you?" the nurse asked John.

"I'm looking for Nurse June Henson. I was told that she worked here in this ward," John said to the nurse.

"This is where June works, but today is her day off, and she went out somewhere with Captain Moore," the nurse told John.

"Do you know when she will be back?" John asked.

"Probably be after tonight. She and that captain usually go to town on their day off," the nurse told John.

"Guess I'll go back to the hotel tonight and come back tomorrow," John said.

"I'll tell her you were here and will come back tomorrow," the nurse told John.

It was late in the afternoon when Josh and his men finished their visit with the patients in the hospitals in Malvern. John was in the bus when the others that spent the day visiting the wounded and sick soldiers came to the bus for the trip back to the hotel in Worcester.

"Everyone go to your room and get ready for dinner. I'll meet you in about thirty minutes, and we will all go to the dining room together," Major Jackson told everyone when they were leaving the bus.

When John and the others entered the dining room in the hotel, all the seating was taken, and a large crowd was standing in the hallway leading to the dining room. The Manager had reserved tables for his special guests at the front of the dining room. Josh and the men that played in his band were wearing their cowboy outfits and had brought their musical instruments along with them to have a short concert for the guests that were dining at the hotel.

"Looks like I'll have to serve a second meal tonight," the Hotel Manager said to Major Jackson.

"Pretty large crowd standing in the hall and lobby," the Major said to the Hotel Manager.

"Do you think if I pay Josh and his men a good sum that they would play for the guests if I serve a second dinner for the evening?" the Hotel Manager asked.

"I'll ask Josh," Major Jackson told the Manager.

After the Major and Josh had a brief talk with all the men in his band, Major Jackson told the Hotel

Manager that they were pretty tired from the all-day visit at the hospitals, but they would play for them if the pay was enough.

"I'll give each of you chaps two pounds if you will do the second concert," the Hotel Manager told Josh.

"What is a pound in good old American dollars?" Josh asked the Manager.

"That would be close to ten US dollars each," the Manager told Josh.

"Not a lot of pay, but we will play for you for three pounds each," Josh said to the Hotel Manager.

"Lot of money, but I'll pay you for the second concert," the Hotel Manager told Josh.

The crowd for the second meal in the dining room was big, and others were waiting in the halls.

"Can't have a third meal tonight. The cooks tell me that they are out of food in the kitchen," the Hotel Manager announced to all that were in the halls hoping to get in.

"May have to come over here in England for a week or two and play in hotels all around if they'll pay us enough," Josh said to the men in his band.

It was after midnight when John and the others in his group were back in their rooms and ready for bed. They could sleep late the next day because the concert for all the military people stationed around Malvern would not be until six o'clock that evening.

John had plans to be up by noon and start walking and hitching a ride back to the hospital in Malvern to visit nurse June Henson.

John's luck was still with him. He only had to walk to the outskirts of the town of Worcester when a GI truck stopped and the driver asked him where he was headed.

"Going up to Malvern where all the hospitals are," John told the truck driver.

"Crawl in the back. Just happened to be bringing supplies up to the hospitals in Malvern," the truck driver told John.

John was still wearing his Army uniform with his Sergeant's stripes. He did this ever since he started his journey at his Mom's house in Canton, North Carolina. This had given him rides and opportunities he would not have had by wearing his civilian clothes.

The truck pulled up to a long white building and the driver stopped its engine. The driver and his helper got out of the truck, and one of them hollered to John, "This is as far as I go. See you later."

The supply building was the first building in the long row of white buildings that were the hospital wards. John had to walk up the hill to the fourth building where he was hoping to find the nurse, June Henson.

When he opened the door to the end of the building where the nurses' station was located, he saw June at the side of a bed where one of the sick soldiers was lying. John stood at the door and waited until June finished whatever she was doing. When she turned and was moving to the next bed, she saw John standing near the door. June left her next patient and came to where John was waiting.

"Good to see you again," June said to John with a big grin on her face.

"What in the world brought you all the way back to England?" June asked John.

"Just wanted to come back to England and visit you and some of the other friends I met over here," John said to June.

"Did Sarah, your wife, come with you?" June asked John.

"Nope. I'm not married," John said to June.

"The last time I saw you, all you could talk about was how you and Sarah were getting married and living somewhere on one of them mountains over on the Thickety side of Canton," June said to John.

"'Druther not talk about that," John said to June.

"I have several more patients to see before I can take a break," June told John. "Take a walk around outside and come back in about an hour, and I'll take a break, and we can visit for a while."

John walked out to the bench where he used to meet Tony when they were patients in the hospital. He was thinking back about Tony losing one of his arms when they were ambushed by the Germans and wondering where he was and what he could be doing. "Must be awful trying to work with only one arm," John was thinking.

Time went by awful slow while John was waiting for the hour to pass and he could have a visit with June and talk about the things that had passed since they last saw each other.

When John came back to the hospital ward, June was waiting at the nurses' station.

"Hope you took good care of your patients," John said to June.

"I take good care of my patients by sending them home soon," June said to John.

"We will have to make this a short visit today. I have to leave in time to go back to the hotel in Worcester before dark," John said to June.

"Why don't you stay here for a few days so we can have a good long talk about our past and maybe a little of what we will be doing in the future," June said to John.

"I'll have Captain Moore get you a room in the Officers Barracks, and you can eat here in the Mess Hall," June said to John.

"That's an awful lot of bother. And besides, I am wearing my Army clothes with the Sergeant marks on the sleeves," John said.

"Won't be no problem. You will be a special visitor here. Come on and we'll meet Tom over at the Surgical Ward," June told John.

June and John left the building where June was the nurse and went to another long white building up the street from them. June was leading the way, and when she opened the door and went in, there was a smell of ether. John was not a nurse or doctor, but the smell of the ether told him that they were in the ward where surgery was being done.

June knew exactly where to go. With John right behind June's heels, they headed to one of the small rooms that the doctors used for keeping their records and studying for their surgeries.

"Hi," June said to a man wearing a long white gown sitting at a small desk.

When he turned his head and saw June, he laid his pencil down on the desk and said, "Hi, Good-looking. What are you doing here in the middle of your workday?"

"Want you to meet a friend of mine that came all the way from North Carolina to visit me," June said to the doctor.

"This is Captain Tom Moore, the head surgeon here in this ward," June said to John as she pointed toward the doctor. "And this is my friend, John Dowdy, all the way from Canton, North Carolina," June said to the Captain.

The Captain and John shook hands, and June gave the Captain a little hug on his shoulder.

"John needs a place to stay for a couple of days. Do you think you could find him a place to sleep in the Officers' Quarters and arrange for him to eat at the Officers' Mess Hall," June asked Captain Moore.

"Shouldn't be any trouble at all. There are a couple of rooms empty. The War is over you know, and people are leaving every week heading back to their homes in the good old USA," Captain Moore said to June and John.

"June can show you where the Officers' Quarters are. I have one more patient to look at today, and then I'll meet you and John in the Mess Hall for dinner," Captain Moore said to June.

June went back to her nursing duties for the rest of the day, and John gave the hospital area a good look outside.

John was sitting at the place where he would visit with Tony when he was a patient after his injures in France when June came out of her ward.

"Hungry, Soldier?" June asked John.

"Always ready to eat," John answered.

When June and John went into the Officers' Mess Hall, Captain Moore was already seated at a table near a small window.

"Saved this table for us. Only place with a view without soldiers," the Captain said to John.

"Haven't mentioned it to you, but Tom and I plan to be married after we finish our hitch here and come home to the good old USA," June said to John.

"I thought that you were engaged to marry that man from the cotton mill in Kings Mountain," John said to June.

"I never told Sam Judson, Junior., that I would marry him. All the arrangements and plans were from Sam Junior and his Dad, Sam Senior," June said to John.

"But your Mom and Dad mentioned something about the wedding when I spent the night with them. What changed the plans?" John asked.

"Let's not talk about weddings and plans. Let's eat, and when we get back to the Officers' Club, I'll tell you all about what has changed since you were here," June said to John.

Tom and John were telling each other about where they lived in the States and what they had been doing after the War ended. June was too busy eating to join in the conversation and was saving her questions for later when John and she would explain to each other why they had never married after the War was over.

When they were finished eating, June said to John, "We'll go over to the Officers' Club and find a quiet corner where we can talk, and I will tell you why I stayed in the Army after the War was over."

It was early in the evening when Tom told June and John that he would go to his room so they could be alone and have a good talk.

June led the way into the Officers' Club looking for a place where she and John could be alone and talk without other people hearing what they were saying. June chose a booth near a window in the room away from the bar where most of the officers gathered to drink and talk.

"Looks like this is about as good as any place to talk," June said to John.

"Looks fine to me," John said.

"We'll keep our voices down, and no one will hear what we are talking about," John said to June.

John and June sat across from each other in the booth. June had an envelope in her hand that she laid on the table near her.

"Don't really know where to start telling you about what has taken place since I last saw you. Guess I'll start at the beginning of my growing up in Kings Mountain," June said to John.

"As you already know, I grew up in the little town of Kings Mountain, North Carolina. Not a large town. Only one cotton mill there and only one high school. A place where everyone knew each other and about most of what they were doing. The cotton mill was the only factory in Kings Mountain. The owner of the mill was a Mr. Sam Judson. He and his wife only had one son. As you would guess, his name would be 'Junior' — Sam Judson, Junior. And as the only child and being the son of the wealthiest family in Kings Mountain, he usual got anything he wanted. That included his friends. Sam Judson, Junior, decided that I would be his best friend — in fact, his girl friend.

"It was in the fifth grade when Sam Junior decided that I would be the one he would marry after we finished school. I didn't dare make him mad because my Dad was the Manager for his Dad's cotton mill. I was afraid that if I made him mad he would find some way to have his Dad fire my Dad. I was in a bind, and I believe Sam Junior knew it.

"All through school I would always receive the most expensive valentines and gifts. Sam Junior could afford them when children from the families that worked in his Dad's cotton mill like George Henson, my Dad, and the other workers had to live on a tight budget.

"There were rumors and talk of a war with Germany when I finished high school, and I told Sam Junior I was going to go to college.

"'We will discuss our future after I finish my schooling,' I said to Sam Junior

"Sam Junior wasn't too happy that he didn't get his way as he had been doing all his life. With his mother on his side of the arguments at home, Sam Junior always won.

"Our country was at war when I graduated from Duke as a licensed registered nurse. The government was asking for doctors and nurses to enlist in the military services. It didn't take me long to decide, so I enlisted for nurse's duty in the Army. This would help my country and also solve my problem of telling Sam Junior that I would never marry him.

"So here I am. I want you to read this letter I received from Sam Junior about a month ago," June said to John as she handed him an envelope marked "private".

John opened the letter and began to read it.

June 12, 1946

Lieutenant June Henson
APO 630 ETO
England

Dear June,

I find myself in a very awkward position searching for words writing this letter to you. I have had many long sleepless nights trying to decide where to start and what to say to you. I've even thought about not letting you hear from me but can't get you out of my mind and the many years we have been the best of friends, and as you remember I was always making plans for you and me to be married. These plans have changed since I last saw you.

I'm sure you know that I didn't go into the military when the War started and every man over the age of eighteen was subject to being drafted if they didn't volunteer or were working somewhere that was needed to help supply materials to those in the War. My Dad kept me from being drafted, and when I mentioned my volunteering for the service, he told me that helping him keep the mill going would be important so there would be cloth to make clothes for the ones in the military service, so I never left home.

I've made all the excuses I know, so here is what has happened since I last saw you or wrote to you. Like I said, I am working with my Dad in his cotton mill. I work in the accounting and payroll department. All the men that did work here are gone, and all the work is being performed by women —women of all ages, sizes, and looks.

    I work next desk to a girl about your age. She has blond hair and is above the average when it comes to pretty. We became very friendly after a few months, and I began to invite her to go eat lunch with me. Later, we began to go to movies and social gatherings—even a few dances at the country club. I never dreamed that there would ever be another girl that could replace you as my future wife, but it happened. Betty (Betty Wells) and I fell in love.

    After about six months, I asked Betty if she would marry me. She said yes, and we were married six months later. We made a trip down to South Carolina where there was no waiting time or physical exams. We never told my parents or hers. It didn't seem to bother my Dad, but my mother pitched a big one about me marrying a working girl. What would her friends in her social clubs say about me marrying a common working girl?

Now that I have told you that our engagement for marriage is off, I feel relieved about having to give you the news. June, I hope that we can still be good friends and that you find someone someday that you fall in love with, and maybe you will marry them.

When you ever come back to Kings Mountain, you have a standing invitation to come visit Betty and me.

I wish you much happiness and health in your future journey through life.

Sincerely,

Sam Judson, Junior

Sam Judson, Jr.
100 Judson Drive
Kings Mountain, North Carolina
USA

When John finished reading the letter June had given him, he looked up and saw June smiling from ear to ear.

"What do you think?" June asked John

"You seem awful happy to have received a 'Dear John' letter from your love back home," John teased.

"What happened to Sarah and your wedding when you returned to North Carolina?" June asked John again.

"I don't want to talk about it, sort of doing like you did. Wait for a spell and let things happen, and then I'll answer your question about Sarah and me," John said to June.

John looked out the window where he and June were sitting and noticed that it was dark.

"Guess we had better call it a day," John said to June.

"Guess so. I have to be at work early tomorrow morning," June said.

"See you at breakfast," June told John as she stood from the table to leave.

John went to the Officers' Quarters and went into the room that his new-found friend, Captain Tom Moore, had made arrangements for him to use while he was visiting June at the hospital. John went to the shower room, took a good bath, and headed straight to his bed. He was tired from the long, all-day visit at the hospital.

John was up and dressed at 0600 so he wouldn't miss Tom and June at the Officers Mess. June had told John that they usually ate breakfast somewhere between 0630 and 0700 when they were scheduled for work that day. When John arrived at the dining room, he found Tom there waiting for June and him to come so they could eat together.

When June arrived, the three of them went to the chow line with June leading the way. The soldiers who were serving the meal had a long look at John as he came through for his breakfast. It seemed sort of strange and out of place that a soldier with sergeant strips was with a captain and nurse lieutenant.

Tom, June, and John sat together, but none of them were very talkative this early in the day. Tom and June also had to hurry off to work.

John told them that he was planning on going to Worcester that day to visit some friends he met while he was at the hospital before returning home after he was wounded.

"I may spend the night at a hotel tonight, so don't you two worry about me," John told Tom and June.

"Be sure and come back," June said to John.

"We didn't finish talking about what has passed since you were here a couple of years ago," June said to John.

"I'll be back tomorrow if it gets too late for me to come back today," John said.

After Tom and June left, John went back to his room , made his bed, and laid his bag on the chair near his bed with all that he had brought along for his journey. He was still wearing his Army uniform with the sergeant stripes on his shoulder. He found that this was the way to dress when hitching a ride.

Worcester

John had walked out of the hospital area and headed down the road toward Worcester. He had only gone a little way when a jeep stopped beside him. John saw that the driver had corporal stripes on his sleeve.

"Where you headed, Sarge?" the Corporal asked John.

"Going over to Worcester to visit some friends," John told the jeep driver.

"You're in luck. That's where I'm headed. Have to pick up a little something for the Captain," the Corporal told John. "Where do you want off at in town?"

"If I can find the hotel, I sort of know my way around from there," John said.

"I'm not in a hurry, and I know my way around here pretty well. I come in here pretty often running errands for the officers," the Corporal told John.

The Corporal pulled the jeep to the curb in front of the hotel and said to John, "May be back here again tomorrow. I never know what the officers want me to pick up for them here in Worcester. Check at the bar on the street below here. The officers always run out of scotch."

"Thanks. I'll watch for you, and if I start walking back from town tomorrow, you keep an eye out for me. Pretty long walk. Riding is lots easier on the feet," John said as he grinned to the Corporal.

John went into the hotel restaurant and asked the clerk at the desk if he could speak to the Hotel Manager.

"And who can I say you are?" the clerk asked John.

"Tell him that the soldier that was with the two Majors and group that did the concert in the dining room would like to talk with him," John said to the hotel clerk.

The hotel clerk picked up his phone and pushed a button. John heard a lady's voice.

"Mr. Cummings' office. May I help you?" The lady asked the clerk.

"There is a soldier here that would like to speak with Mr. Cummings," the clerk said.

After a short pause, the lady on the phone said to the hotel clerk, "Send him to my office."

The clerk hung up the phone and began to tell John how he could find Mr. Cummings' office.

John didn't have any trouble finding the office, and he opened the door and went in. He didn't see the Hotel Manager. There was a pretty young lady sitting behind a desk. She smiled and pointed her finger to a door behind her.

"Open the door and go in. Mr. Cummings is waiting for you," the secretary said to John.

When John opened the door and entered, Mr. Cummings, the Hotel Manager, got up from his desk and held out his hand toward John. John reached out and shook the Hotel Manager's hand.

"Good to see you again, Soldier," the Manager said as he shook John's hand. "I hope you have news of Josh and his Tennessee Walkers."

"I haven't heard from them since they left for concerts for the military personnel in France and Germany. Don't know if they will drop back by here on their way back to Tennessee," John said.

"Wish they would so Josh and his men could do another show for me here at the hotel," the Manager said.

"I hope so, too. I will be needing a ride back to North Carolina any day now. I'm here to visit some friends I met when I was here a few years ago and was wondering if you could let me have a room for tonight?" John told the Hotel Manager.

"Sure can, and it is on me. Won't cost you a shilling," he said to John.

"Come by before dinner is served, and we will have something to eat together and have a good chat," the Manager told John.

"I'd better get going to visit and be back in time to eat with you," John said as he and the Manager shook hands again.

As John was walking down the street toward the restaurant where he and Tony used to eat fish-and-chips dinners, he couldn't believe the good luck he had since leaving his home in Canton, North Carolina. He had spent only a little of the money he had in his money belt around his belly under his shirt.

John didn't have any trouble finding the restaurant and opened the door not knowing who he would see after being away for almost two years. When John went into the restaurant, a young lady was standing at the door. She had a menu in her hand and gave John a big smile.

"Do you have any special place you would like to sit?" she asked John.

"Don't know yet. I want to look around for a few minutes," John told the hostess.

"Are you expecting someone to meet you here?" she asked John.

"A friend and I were here nearly three years ago, and two of the waitresses here waited on us. One was named Jane, and the other was Pam. Do they still work here?" John asked.

"Don't know of anyone by the name of Jane, but the Manager here is a lady, and her given name is Pam. Would she be the one you are looking for?" she asked.

"Don't know until I see her," John answered.

"I'll go let her know that you would like to see her," she said to John.

When the restaurant Manager came in, both John and Pam spoke at the same time.

"John. You are back," Pam said with a big smile on her face.

"Pam, been a long time," John said.

"Come in the office where we can talk about what we have done for the last several years," Pam told John.

"The last time I saw you was when you and Jane were our waitresses when Tony and I ate our first fish-and-chips dinner," John said to Pam.

Pam led the way as she and John went into a fancy, paneled office with a big desk in the middle of the room.

"Awful fancy room you have here," John said as he was looking around her desk.

"Only had this job a little over six months. The man that was the manager from the start of this restaurant was over eighty years old and decided it was time to retire. He recommended to the owners that I should take the manager's position," Pam told John.

"Where is Jane, the girl that was with you when I was here?" John asked Pam.

"Nearly tea time, so what do you say we have something brought here in the office, and I'll tell you about her," Pam said.

Pam pushed a button on her desk, and the waitress came in.

"We would like something to eat," Pam said to the young lady.

The waitress took a pencil from behind her ear and a pad out of the pocket in her little apron.

"What can I get for you?" She asked Pam.

"I'll have tea and a sweet roll. What do you want, John?" Pam said.

"Do you have iced tea?" John asked the waitress.

She looked at John and then Pam.

Pam smiled and said to John, "We don't drink our tea with ice and lemon here like you Americans do. It is always hot, and there is sugar and milk if you want it in your tea." Pam smiled at John.

"Guess I'll have the same as you," John said to Pam.

John sat in a chair near the desk where Pam was sitting in a big soft chair behind her desk.

"You asked me about where Jane is now. The truth is, I can't say. All I know is that she sure got herself in a mess shortly after you were here," Pam said.

"What happened?" John asked.

"Jane was a little older than me. I was a little over seventeen years old, and I guess she was a little above twenty. There was a soldier from the hospital up near Malvern that come by here a lot and ate fish-and-chips. He always wanted Jane to be his waitress and always gave her a big tip. He would hang around until Jane finished her work for the day, and the two of them would go off somewhere. She never told me where they went or what they did, and I never tried to pick it out of her.

"About a month later, Jane told me she was quitting her work here. She said that she and Frank were going to be married and would be moving to America when he was discharged from the Army. She told me that Frank had rented a flat, and they would live there until leaving for America. I didn't see her again until I accidentally met her in a shop where I was buying some food. I spoke to her and could see that she was very fat.

"Pam, I wish I were dead," she said to me as tears ran down her cheeks.

"'Don't say things like that,' I said.

"Well, I do. Look at me," she cried as she put her arms around me.

"What has happened to you?" I asked her.

Jane began and told me her story:

"You remember how happy I was the day I told you the news about Frank and me getting married and living in America. And we rented a flat, and we lived together but were not married. Take a look at me and, you will know what happened.

"But you should be happy that you and Frank will have children," I told her.

Jane went on and told me that she hadn't seen Frank and didn't know where he was. He disappeared as soon as he found out that she was going to have a baby. She went to the hospital where he was supposed to be working and was told he had moved. She did find out that he was from New York, and his name was Frank Forgy. That is all they would tell her. She was desperate and had to go back to her Mom and Dad. She couldn't get a job to pay the rent on the flat.

"That was the last I heard from Jane. It was so sad," Pam told John.

"Sure wished there was something I could do to help her. She and you were so nice to Tony and me at the restaurant," John said to Pam.

"What happened with you and that girl you were always talking about? I believe you called her Sarah," Pam said to John.

"Things didn't work out like it was planned, and I had rather forget about her," John told Pam.

"What about you? Are you married now?" John asked Pam.

"No, not yet, but I will be a fortnight after David finishes his military requirement. He has nearly three more months. David and I attended school together, so we know each other pretty well. I don't think he will do to me what that Frank Forgy rat did to Jane," Pam told John.

"Sure wished I would have come here sooner. I may have asked you to marry me," John said.

Pam blushed and said, "And I may have said yes."

Pam and John finished drinking their tea, and Pam said to John, "Why don't you come back this evening, and you and I will have high tea together."

"What in the world is high tea?" John asked.

Pam laughed and said, "Some Americans call it 'dinner', but I believe the people that come from the mountains call it 'supper'."

"What time?" John asked.

"Around six this evening," Pam answered.

Pam and John were at the restaurant and ready for 'high tea' at six that evening. They did more talking about what their dreams and wishes for their future were than eating.

"May take a holiday some time, when David and I can go, all the way to North Carolina in America to visit. You will probably have a wife by then," Pam told John.

"That would be great for you to come visit. And, as you said, I may find someone that will make me a good wife. I haven't stopped looking," John said.

Pam and John had finished their supper. Pam mentioned it was getting late in the evening. They hadn't realized they had talked so long.

"Guess you and I better call it a day and head for home. You will be working tomorrow, and I plan to pay another visit to the hospital before I head back home to North Carolina," John said to Pam.

They gave each other a farewell hug, and John said to Pam, "Sure wish I had come back here before you and David planned to be married. I'll be looking for your visit when you take a vacation or, as you say, your 'holiday'."

"Good luck, and have a nice trip back home," Pam said as they left the restaurant.

John went directly to the hotel and straight to bed. He was going back to the hospital up at Malvern, and he didn't know if he would hitch a ride. He may have to walk all the way, and this would talk at least a half of the day. He wanted to talk with June and Tom about how he could find transportation back to the United States. Once he was there, he wouldn't have any problems hiking to Fort Bragg and then on to Canton. He had promised his old Sergeant to come back and see him again before he returned back home.

John was up early, ate a quick breakfast, and asked the desk clerk at the hotel to tell the Manager he would stop by again before leaving for home.

He gathered his belongings together and was on his way to the hospital up at Malvern.

He had been on the road for over an hour, and all he saw was someone on a bicycle or walking. He was hoping that one of the American trucks would come by and give him a ride.

The sun was up, and John was beginning to tire from his long walk. Near the forks of the main road to Malvern, there was a tall building with a sign that said, "Half Way House". He saw a couple of older men enter the building and decided that he should see what was in this house.

He opened the door, and when he entered it didn't take John long to see what they sold there. It was one of the many Pubs. Although he had never visited the bars back home, he knew that this was what he always called, a 'beer joint'. His Mom had told him about these places and told him to stay away from them.

There were a couple of older men sitting at a table drinking some kind of brown liquid. At the end of the room there were another two men that looked about the ages of the ones at the table. One of them was throwing bright colored feathers with a long sharp pin at a board that had a bull's-eye circle on it.

"Hi, Soldier. Care for a pint of ale?" the man that was behind the bar said to John.

"No thank you. I just stopped by to rest a little. Quite a walk from Worcester, and from what I see on the building sign, I am only half-way to Malvern," John said to the man behind the long bar.

"I would like a glass of water," John said.

The bartender smiled and said to John, "Don't have any water decent enough to drink, but I do have a bottle of ginger ale if you want something besides beer or spirits."

"The ginger ale will be fine," John said.

The bartender noticed that John was very curious about the men at the end of the room throwing the feathers with the sharp nails at the bulls-eye.

"Care for a game of darts," he asked John.

"Never played it, but it does look a little challenging," John answered.

The bartender walked from behind the bar and motioned for John to come with him.

"These are my friends, Bill and Henry. The best dart players at the Half Way House. How about showing this soldier how to play darts," he said to the two dart players.

The older player explained to John about the game of darts:

"Hold the dart in your hand like this. Take a good aim, and hit the center of the target. Here. Give it a try," he said as he handed John a hand-full of darts.

John held his hand above his shoulder, squinted his left eye, and threw the dart toward the target. It hit in the center of the bulls-eye.

The two dart players looked at each other then at the dart board.

"Are you sure you never played this game before?" the older man asked John.

"First time I ever had one in my hand," John answered as he handed the other darts to his instructor.

John finished drinking his ginger-ale drink, set the bottle on the table, and said to the bartender.

"Better be on my way. How much do I owe you for the drink?" John asked.

"Nothing. On the house. And thanks for teaching my buddies the way to throw a dart," the bartender said as he smiled toward the two players near the dartboard.

John had not walked too far when he heard the sound of a truck. He knew that it was an American vehicle, and when he turned to look, there was a six-by-six coming his way. He stopped and faced the truck so the driver could see that he was an American. The truck stopped, and the driver hollered to John, "Want a ride, Soldier?"

"Sure do. Been walking all morning. On my way to the hospital up at Malvern," John told the driver.

"Just happen to be going up there. Hop in," the truck driver said.

The driver and John didn't do much talking as they drove up the road to the hospital area. Just the usual small talk about where they were from and when they would be going back to the States.

When the truck came into the area where all the buildings belonging to the hospital camp were, the driver stopped the truck in front of a building with a sign saying, "Supply Warehouse".

"Here we are soldier," he said to John.

"Thanks for the ride. I know my way from here," John told the truck driver.

John went to the Officers' Quarters and the room that Tom had made arrangements for him to sleep in while he was there to visit June. He would meet them that evening when she and Tom came to eat supper.

John went into the dining room at the Mess Hall a little after five and sat at the window where he and June were the evening she showed him the letter she received from her long-time school friend from Kings Mountain. June and Tom came into the Mess Hall about the same time. Tom saw John sitting near the window and tapped June on the shoulder and pointed to John. They come over and sat next to him.

"Good to see you back," June said to John.

"Only gone for one day. Just wanted to see some friends in Worcester before I head back to North Carolina," John said.

"When we finish our supper, I need advice from you two," John said to Tom and June.

As the three ate they talked about what they would be doing after they were married, like where they would make their homes and how Tom would open his own clinic to be a family doctor. And maybe June would be his nurse for a year or so before having any children. They were excited about their plans for their future.

When the orderly took the dishes away from the table, Tom said to John, "What do you want to ask us?"

"Well, it's about advice on what would be the best way for me to get back to the US," John told him.

"Guess the best way would be to go to one of the docks where the ships sail to New York from here. June and I will be going that way," Tom said.

"That's what I've been thinking, but don't know which port to find one at," John said to Tom.

"Our ship will be leaving from Southampton. The Transportation Officer told me most all of their ships sailed from there," Tom said.

"Guess I'll take a train tomorrow to Southampton and see what I can arrange," John said.

"The soldiers here get to ride for free on the trains, and maybe you still do, so you will have that part of your trip solved," Tom said.

"Guess I'll tell you two goodbye and leave early tomorrow morning. I'll have to try and hitch a ride to Worcester to catch the train to Southampton," John told Tom and June.

"I'll have a driver take you to the train station in Worcester as soon as you have your breakfast. A man can't travel very well on an empty stomach," Tom said to John.

"See you at breakfast," June said as she and Tom were leaving.

John didn't' sleep too well that night, as he lay thinking of how he would get across the wide ocean to the US and then on to Canton, North Carolina. "I'll find a way," he said to himself as he fell asleep.

John was in the dining room at the Mess Hall when Tom and June came in for breakfast.

"You need some identification to show that you were in the military service," Tom said to John.

"I have my Army discharge papers with me. They have some records of my service, such as the purple heart and medals I earned," John told Tom.

"Guess that will do, but I made you an identification card last night showing the address of this hospital location. If you are asked for some identity when you get on the train, show them this card," Tom said as he handed the card to John.

They had finished eating breakfast and were saying goodbye when a soldier came in and told Tom he was ready to leave for Worcester.

"See you in North Carolina in about three months," June said to John.

John didn't talk very much as they were on the way to the train station in Worcester. He was sad at leaving his good friends and giving a lot of thought as to how he would get back to the States.

"Good luck, Sergeant," the driver said as John got out of the Jeep.

"Thanks for the ride," John answered.

Journey Home

John went into the ticket office in the train station and asked a Ticket Clerk when the next train would be going to Southampton.

"A train leaves for London in thirty minutes. You will have to board another train in London to the port of Southampton," the Ticket Clerk told John.

"Need to see your ID card," the Ticket Clerk said to John.

John handed him the card that Tom had made for him. The Ticket Clerk looked at it and handed it back along with another card.

"This should get you all the way to the port at Southampton," he told John.

John went onto the platform where people were boarding a train. He asked the Conductor checking tickets if this was the train to London.

"Sure is. Can I see your pass?"

John handed the Conductor the card he received from the Ticket Clerk.

"Have a nice ride," the Conductor told John.

John walked through the walkway inside the train where there were doors all along. When he opened one of the doors, there were two long seats facing each other. In one of the seats there were a well-dressed man and woman. John sat opposite them on the other seat. In a few minutes the carriage compartment had eight people on the two seats. Two more men and lady couples and one English soldier had sat down. These would be John's riding companions all the way to London.

As the train was leaving the station, the English soldier asked John where he was going.

"To Southampton," John told him.

"So am I," the soldier told John.

"What brings you to Southampton?" The English soldier asked.

"I need a way back to the US, and I'm hoping I will find a ship that I can go on. Would be a long swim, and besides I am afraid of water," John joked to the soldier.

"My name is Bayles— Lance Corporal Bayles. I'm stationed at a camp that helps the war brides and their children get transportation to the States to join their husbands. Many Americans married English girls during their stay here for World War

II. In fact, there is a ship due to sail to America in about one week. I believe its name is the *Henry Gibbons*. A troop transfer that was remodeled to accommodate the needs of women and children," Corporal Bayles told John.

"Great. That sounds like what I'm looking for," John said.

John and the Corporal went up front of the train coach where there were tables and seats. They had the waiter bring them tea and cookies. As usual with English tea, it was hot and there was sugar and cream. John only had sugar in his.

"Do you know anyone that I could talk with about hitching a ride back to the US?" John asked as they were drinking their tea.

"Our camp is close to the docks, and some of our offices are shared with the Americans that take care of the ships," Corporal Bayles told John.

The train pulled into the station in London, and the Conductor announced that everyone would have to get off. The Corporal had made this trip several times and knew where to take John for the remainder of the ride to Southampton. He led the way, and soon he and John were in their train going to the docks on the English Channel.

John began to close his eyes and drop his head. The clicking of the rails on the train was making him sleepy. He didn't sleep very well the night before leaving for this trip. Soon he was sound asleep sitting in his seat on the train. He awoke when the English soldier shook his shoulder and said, "Wake up, Yank. We're nearing the station for Southampton."

"I'll show you to the docks where the ships are anchored when we leave the station," the Corporal said.

John and the English soldier were walking toward the area where the large ships were docked. Corporal Bayles pointed toward a large white ship and said to John, "There she is, the *Henry Gibbons*. That's the ship I was telling you about."

John shook the Corporal's hand and thanked him for telling him about the ship. He headed straight to the stairs where he saw people walking toward the ship. When he reached the top of the walkway, an MP motioned to John.

"Need to see your ID," he said to John.

He handed his Army discharge papers to the MP and said, "I need to talk to whoever is in charge of letting people on this ship."

"That would be Major Anderson. That's him standing to your right. I'll motion him to come over here," the MP said.

Major Anderson came to where John was standing and said, "What do you want Sergeant?"

"I'm a long way from home and need a ride back to the States," John said as he handed his discharge papers to the Major.

The Major looked at the papers and said to John, "I see that you were discharged from the Army over three years ago at Fort Bragg, North Carolina. What in the Sam Hill are you doing way over here?"

"Well Major, when I was discharged I went to my home in Canton, North Carolina, and was planning on marrying my long-time girlfriend. When I found her she was already married. I hitch-hiked to Kings Mountain where the nurse that looked after me when I was wounded over in France came from. She didn't come back after the War was over. June reenlisted and stayed over here in England.

"I went to Fort Bragg and worked there for over a year then bummed a ride to England on a plane bringing some entertainers over for a USO show. When I found June, she was engaged to a doctor, a Captain at the hospital. I'm on my way back to North Carolina and need a ride," John told the Major.

"Sure is a small world," the Major said.

"I was born and raised in Kings Mountain. My Dad worked in the only factory in town, a cotton mill. Who was that girl, June, you mentioned?" The Major asked.

"June Henson. Her Dad was George Henson. He worked in the cotton mill." John answered.

"Knew the Henson family well. My Dad and George worked together. And I remember a little skinny girl with freckles in the second grade the year I left for college. Is she still skinny?" the Major asked.

"You must be mistaken about June. She is a very pretty girl, and Mother Nature has been good to her. No sir, June is not the girl you saw when you were in school," John told the Major.

"Come with me," the Major said to John. "I'll see if I can crowd in another passenger."

John followed the Major into a room and down some stairs into a room where several Army and Navy officers were sitting at desks. They stopped at a desk where a Major was sitting.

"Major, Sergeant Dowdy is a friend of mine, and he needs a ride back to the States. Think you can find a place for him?" Major Anderson asked.

"Always room for one of your friends," the Major at the desk said.

He opened a ledger type book and scanned down the pages with his fingers and stopped. He looked at John and asked him what his name was.

"John Dowdy, Staff Sergeant, US Army," he said.

"You will be in room six on "C" deck. Here are the times for meal servings," the Major said as he handed John some papers.

"Thanks, Major," John said as he saluted the Major and left.

"And thank you, Major Anderson. I hope I can visit you when you get back to Kings Mountain," John said.

"We will raise anchor and be on our way day after tomorrow. Take a walk around and get acquainted, and I'll look you up before we get to New York," Major Anderson said.

After John was settled in his room, he wandered around and located the dining room where he was assigned to eat while on the ship.

John was taking a nap after supper on the second day he was on the ship when he was awakened by the humming of engines and the feeling that his bed was moving. He stood and looked out of a porthole and saw the docks moving by. He was on his way back home.

For the next several days John spent most of his time on the deck looking at passing ships and other things that passed by. He also had plenty of time to think about what may happen in his future after he got back to Canton. He also made plans to stop by Fort Bragg and see his old Sergeant one more time. He closed his eyes and gave thanks for all the good things that had happened since he left home. He always remembered what his Mom told him while growing up, "John, don't ever get too busy to stop and thank our Maker for watching over us and the many blessings He gives you." John never forgot that advice.

The eight-day ocean journey seemed slow to John, but it was gradually ending. On the eighth morning while looking toward the direction they were moving, John began to see lots of sea birds, and he saw some dolphins swimming alongside of the ship. He squinted his eyes, and in the distance he got a glimpse of what looked like a statue.

"Must be the Statue of Liberty," John said to a soldier and girl beside him.

"Won't be long until we'll be docking in New York," the soldier said to John.

John hadn't seen Major Anderson since the day he met him. He went to his room, gathered his belongings together, and began to try and find him. He went to the office area where he was assigned a place to stay and saw Major Anderson at a desk in the back of the room. He seemed real busy looking through a pile of papers, but John went to where he was and said to him, "Major Anderson, I had to see you and tell you how much I appreciate you getting me back home again. If I find out when you retire and come back to Kings Mountain, I'll come visit you."

"You are welcome, Sergeant. Glad to help an old Tar Heel. Sorry I didn't get to see you on the way over, but have been real busy this trip. You take care, and I hope you find that girl you are looking for."

John saluted the Major and left.

John was waiting on deck near the place where the steps would be lowered for getting off the ship. He was anxious to get back on the solid ground of the good old USA.

A tugboat pushed the ship into position at the pier where a longshoreman motioned where to drop anchor. When the ship was alongside, they were tied to the dock with very large ropes. The steps were lowered and ready for the passengers to get off the ship. John wasn't the first one off, but he was not far behind the deck hands that checked to be sure it was safe to start the unloading.

Once John was ashore, he asked one of the men working on the deck where the bus and train stations were. He was anxious to get on his way to Fort Bragg for a short visit with the Sergeant and then head for his home in Canton. His first stop was the train station and to the ticket booth.

"When will the next train be leaving for Fort Bragg, North Carolina?" John asked the man at the booth.

He moved his finger over a list of numbers on a card on the wall and said, "The Southern Bell will be leaving on track six at nine this morning. That is about an hour from now."

"How much is the ticket?" John asked.

After looking again at the papers before him the man said, "That will be fourteen dollars and fifty cents."

John opened his shirt and reached inside and pulled some money from his money belt around his waist. He handed the money to the ticket man and said, "Give me a ticket to Fayetteville, North Carolina. That's where the train station is."

When the ticket clerk had handed him the ticket, he headed toward where the trains were, looking for his ride— train number six.

He found the train but was told it would be another ten minutes before he could get on. The waiting time seemed like hours to John. He was in a hurry to be on his way.

He took a seat near the window and watched as the black smoke rose from the steam engine. He knew it wouldn't be much longer because there was more smoke coming from the smoke stack.

It wasn't long until someone was sitting in all the seats. A man with gray hair wearing a suit took the seat beside John. They didn't speak to each other. John looked out the window, and the man looked around to the other passengers on the train.

The train gave a little jerk and began to move forward. The gray headed man beside John said, "'Bout time they get started."

"How many stops will we have before we get to North Carolina?" John asked the man beside him.

"Not many. Only about three, I think. This is the Florida special train. I ride down there at least once every year."

The clicking of the wheels on the steel rails was making John sleepy. He closed his eyes and dozed off to sleep.

John and the man that was sharing the seat with him didn't do a lot of talking on their ride to North

Carolina. They exchanged names and where their home was, watched the fields and small towns pass by, took short naps, and day-dreamed. The train only made two short stops before the next one that would be Fayetteville, North Carolina. This would be where John would get off and head for the Army base of Fort Bragg. John was anxious to see his good friend Sergeant Davis.

John stopped the train conductor that was checking the passengers and asked him how much longer it would be before the train would be at Fayetteville. He took a big gold watch from the pocket on his vest and said, "Just a little over an hour."

It seemed like days for that last hour to go by, and when the train was slowing down to stop at the station, John already had his bag in his hand and was ready to get off as soon as the train stopped moving. He wished the man that sat in the seat near him a pleasant trip on his way to Florida. When the train was still, John headed to the door toward the station.

John didn't waste any time getting on the road to the Fort. He didn't start thumbing the trucks and cars that came by until he was out of the city of Fayetteville.

Sad News

A six-by-six truck pulled to the curb, and the driver hollered to John, "Want a ride, Soldier?"

"Sure do," John said.

As John got in the seat near the driver he said to him, "Hope you are going near the main gate."

"Only way in there," the driver said.

The truck stopped at the guard post. John thanked the driver and got out. He went to the MP on duty, showed him his Army discharge papers, and told him he was here to visit his old Sergeant he had when he took Basic Training.

"Sergeant Brad Davis. The best noncom in the Army," John said to the MP.

"Do you mean the Sergeant that used a walker and was in charge of the Guest House?" the MP said to John.

"That's him. My best friend, Sergeant Brad Davis."

"Hate to tell you, but Sergeant Davis is in the post hospital. I'll have one of my buddies drive you over there," the MP told John.

John was shocked by the news about his good friend Sergeant Davis. He didn't say a word all the way to the hospital.

The Jeep stopped at the emergency door of the hospital, and John was nearly in a run to the door. He went to the desk and asked about Sergeant Brad Davis.

The nurse at the desk looked at the list on her desk and said, "Sergeant Davis is a very sick man. I'll have to ask the doctor if it will be OK for you to visit him."

She picked up the phone and talked to someone. In a few minutes a man dressed in white with something hanging around his neck came to where John had sat down.

"The nurse said you wanted to visit Sergeant Davis. Is he one of your relatives?" the doctor asked.

"No, he doesn't have any known living relatives. I'm his best friend, and he is expecting me to come see him. I promised him I would be here before I went back home. I've been over to England," John told the doctor.

"Come on. I'll go with you," the doctor said.

When the doctor opened the door, Sergeant Davis rose up in his bed and said, "John, you did come back."

The doctor said to John, "I'll leave and let you two be alone. Bet you have a lot to talk about that I don't need to hear," the doctor said to the two Army buddies.

"What are you doing in here?" John asked Sergeant Davis.

"Been feeling kind of puny and checked in to sick call. They took some blood from my arm, and when the doctor looked at it he sent me here to the hospital for some other tests. He told me that something was wrong with my liver, and there was nothing he could do to make it well again. Said all I could do was stay here and rest as much as I can. The doctor didn't tell me I would be well again. The way I see it, he's letting me stay here until I die," Sergeant Davis told John.

"Don't talk like that," John said.

Sergeant Davis didn't answer John. He pulled out a big brown envelope and handed it to him.

"I didn't know if I would be here when you came back, and I had something more to talk about with you. I have it all here in this folder, and when I pass away, I want you to open it and do what I have requested. I also gave the doctor a letter telling what my last wishes are after I am dead," Sergeant Davis said to John.

John again asked the Sergeant to not talk like that.

The doctor came back into the room and told John he had better leave.

"The Sergeant needs to rest. You can come back tomorrow morning and visit him," he said to John.

John took his old buddy's hand and said, "Hang in there, Sarge. I'll see you bright and early tomorrow."

As John was leaving, he asked the doctor if there was someone that would give him a ride to the Guest House on base.

"They keep an MP on duty here around the clock. I'll have one of them to give you a ride."

John went to the room he had before leaving for England. He stored the envelope that his Sergeant had given him in his pack with his clothes. Tears come into his eyes as he thought about what the Sergeant had said about him staying in the hospital until he died.

The night went very slow, and John didn't sleep hardly any at all. He couldn't get it off his mind about what was happening to his best friend.

He was up and at the Mess Hall before they started serving breakfast. He sat at a table and waited until the food was ready. He didn't eat but a little of his breakfast and left to go to the hospital. Again, he hitched a ride with one of the MPs.

John went to the desk and asked if he could visit Sergeant Brad Davis. The nurse on duty slid her finger down the list showing the names and locations of the patients. She went over the list again and told John that she didn't have anyone listed by that name.

"I was here last night and talked with him," John told the nurse.

She picked up the telephone and dialed someone. She asked about Sergeant Davis and then hung up the telephone.

"I have sad news for you. Your friend Sergeant Davis is in the morgue. He passed away last night," the nurse said.

"Can I talk with someone at the morgue?" John asked.

The nurse picked up the telephone and called someone. When she hung up the telephone, she told John the directions to the morgue and told him that a doctor would meet him there.

When John got to the room, he saw a sign above the door: "MORGUE". A man wearing a long white coat was waiting for John.

"I am Doctor Marcos. The nurse told me you wanted to talk to me about Brad Davis."

"Yes. My name is John Dowdy. I'm not related to the Sergeant, but I was the only one close to him. He didn't have any living relatives, and I am the only close friend he had. I would like to make the arrangements for his funeral," John said.

"Sergeant Davis had his arrangements made as he wished several days before he died. He requested that his body be cremated and the ashes scattered in the yard of his old barracks. He didn't want anything else — no mourning, visitors, or announcements about him dying. You should go on home and honor his last wishes," the Doctor told John.

Tears ran down John's cheeks as he left the hospital walking up the street toward the Guest House where he would get his belongings and continue his journey back home to Canton. He was sad when his Army buddies were killed in WW II, but not as sad as he was for his long-time friend Sergeant Brad Davis. He took out his handkerchief and dried his eyes and began looking for a ride back to the Guest House.

"I'm glad I got back in time to see him before he died," John said to himself.

BACK HOME

John went directly to his room in the Guest House and packed his bag. He didn't want to spend another night at Fort Bragg now that his good friend Sergeant Davis was gone. With his belongings packed, he started toward the main entrance to the Fort hoping someone would give him a ride. No one gave him a ride, and he had to walk all the way to the guard station. He asked the MP on duty if he knew where he could get a ride to Fayetteville.

"The post bus will be by in about five minutes. You can ride it into town, but they will charge you twenty five cents," the MP said.

There would no more hitching rides to return back to Canton. He still had money in his money belt. He would get on the bus in Fayetteville going to Asheville then take another to Canton.

When the post bus arrived in town, John went directly to the bus station. He went to the ticket window and asked the clerk when the next bus would be going to Asheville.

The clerk looked at the schedules and told John that the bus to Charlotte was due in twenty minutes, and he would have to change buses there to the one going to Asheville.

John didn't ask how much the ticket would cost as he usually did. He just told the clerk that he wanted the ticket for all the way to Canton, North Carolina.

The bus was on time, and John found him a seat near the back of the bus. He wanted to be alone and not be bothered when the riders came on and off the bus.

Once the bus was on the road, the hum of the engine soon had John is a trance. He couldn't keep his eyes open and was soon asleep. The frequent stops the bus made along the road to Charlotte didn't wake him. He hadn't slept very much since he visited Sergeant Davis at the hospital the night before he died.

The connections for the bus from Charlotte to Asheville and on to Canton were good. John didn't have but a short wait between his bus rides.

It was late in the evening when the bus stopped at the station. John stretched himself and headed toward 1520 North Main Street where his Mom and Dad lived. He was anxious to see his family after being away for over two years.

It was nearly dark when John walked to the door and knocked. His Mom opened the door and let out a loud, "John, you're back home!" She gave him a big hug, and they went into the room where his Dad was sitting. He laid his paper down and grabbed John's hand.

"Welcome home, Son," his Dad said.

"Your brother is at work. He is working the second shift in the paper mill. Your sisters are off in school. Betty is training to be a school teacher. Beth, your youngest sister, wants to be a nurse when she finishes school. I'm real proud of all my children for their upbringing and getting out of that life on the top of Little Sam.

"Guess we better get to bed. Soon be time to cook breakfast," John's Mom said.

John was up and sitting in the kitchen talking to his Mom while she was cooking breakfast. His Dad came in and took his usual seat at the long dining table. John's Mom placed biscuits, ham, saw-mill gravy, eggs, apple sauce, and several types of jelly on the table. His Dad said the blessing, and John dug in to the best meal he had eaten since he had left home. His brother stayed in bed. He had worked in the paper mill until midnight.

After everyone finished eating, John's Dad left for the paper mill where he worked, and his Mom finished cleaning the kitchen. John went to his bedroom. He took everything out of his pack and laid it on his bed. There was the large envelope that Sergeant Davis had given him before he died. He held it in his hands for a few minutes and stared at it. "John Dowdy — Personal and Private", he saw printed on it. He hesitated before opening it. He took a letter from inside and began to read:

19 January 1947

To my best friend, John Dowdy,

I wanted to tell you what I am about to write you when we first talked about the girl I was in love with over in Tennessee. I never told you that after she married, Captain Jack Henderson divorced her and transferred to Germany. She wrote me a letter asking if I would forgive her and come back to Oak Ridge and marry her. I never answered her letter. I just began drinking. I was bitter and hard-headed.

John, that was the biggest mistake I ever made. If I had swallowed my pride and gone back to Betty, we would have married, and I would still be alive with a family and have a happy home.

You never told me about why you never married the girl you were in love with. I believe you called her Sarah. The name doesn't mean anything. Just take some advice from someone who made a big mistake. If something like what happened to me should happen to you, don't be a fool like I was. Swallow your pride and give her and yourself another chance.

John paused his reading for a few seconds and began to read on:

John, in the small white envelope you will find a certified check for the amount of seventeen thousand, three hundred and fifty dollars. This was all the money in my savings account that I have saved since being in the Army. I have no other family, and I want you, my friend and only family, to have this money. Take it and build the house you were always talking about. Fulfill your dream of having a house on Little Sam Mountain. These are my wishes, so please do as I have written.

It was a blessing for you to come my way. You were the only happiness I ever knew. Goodbye, my friend.

Brad Davis

John folded the letter. Tears were running down his cheeks as he cried. He wiped the tears from his eyes and placed the letter with the check back into the large folder. He then went back to the room where his Mom was sweeping the floor.

"Do you want to take a walk up on the mountain and look over the place where I plan to build my house?" John asked his Mom.

"As soon as I finish cleaning and get this apron off," she replied.

About an hour later, John and his Mom were pointing to where the house should sit. John suggested that the front porch should be close to the steep side of the mountain, but his Mom said it would be best a little farther up the hill near where the spring was, and John agreed with her.

"Got to borrow a horse and sled to haul all of them gray rocks out of the field. I'll pile them up over there so the people that build my house for me can use them for the foundation," John told his Mom.

After they returned to the house on Main Street, John told his Mom that he would go tomorrow and talk with the lumber supply store and ask about getting someone to build his house. He never mentioned to anyone how he would pay for the house. Everyone only knew that he owned the land on Little Sam Mountain.

After breakfast the next morning, John asked his Mom where the lumber store was. She gave him the directions, and off he headed searching for someone to build his house on Little Sam Mountain.

"Can I help you?" the man at the desk asked John when he came in the door at the lumber yard.

"I am planning to build a house and need to know if you have someone that would build it for me and how much it would cost," John said.

"It depends on what kind of house you build. Do you have any plans?" he asked John.

"I don't have any plans, but I know what I would like the house to look like," John said.

The man at the desk reached down behind the counter and handed John some books with house plans in them.

"See if you find something you would like," he said to John.

After looking over several plans, John pointed to one of them and said, "This sort of looks like what I want. One long room all the way in the back for the kitchen and dining room with a chimney for the cook stove. A hall with two bedrooms on one side and one large bedroom on the other side. On the end, I want a large sitting room with a big rock chimney and a porch all across the house. And I want plenty of glass windows in the rooms. And tin on the roof."

"I have four good carpenters that build for me. If you will go with one of them and show him where you want the house, I can give you a cost for materials and labor," the supply man told John.

The carpenter that went with John to see where the house would be had a car, and they rode to the top of the road where the wagon road led to the spot for the house.

"Guess you will want a rock foundation under the house," the carpenter said to John.

"Over there is a pile of rocks you can use, and if you need more, I'll bring you some more out of the field," John said.

When they returned to the lumber store, the supply man said to John, "You come back tomorrow, and I will tell you what it will cost you and how long it will take to build this house."

The next morning John returned to the lumber store and agreed on the cost with the lumber company.

"We'll get started first thing next Monday," the store owner told John.

John went everyday and watched as the workers were building his house. After three weeks passed, he was watching the workers putting on a shiny tin roof.

Sarah

As John watched, the builders were making a lot of noise with the tin roof. Someone pecked him on the leg. When he looked down, there stood a little boy looking up at him.

"My name is John," the small boy said to John.

John squatted down, put his hand on the little boy's shoulder and said, "Where in the world did you come from?"

The boy pointed to the wagon road that came to where the house was being built. When John looked around he saw Sarah standing under a tree beside the road. He looked back to the little boy that said his name was John and asked, "Don't she know the way up here?"

"She brought me for you to see," the little boy said.

"Go tell her to come on here. I won't bite her," John told his new-found friend.

Little John ran as fast as his little legs would carry him. He reached out and pulled Sarah by the arm and said, "Come see the house. He won't bite you."

Sarah held his hand and walked to where John was standing.

"Hi Sarah," John said. "Is this your little boy?"

"Yes, this is John. I named him after you. I wanted you to see him," Sarah said.

"How did you know I was back home? I've been gone for over two years," John said.

"I saw your mother at the grocery store last week, and I asked her if you were still gone. She told me about you building your house up on Little Sam. I've told John about you and how you went far away in the War. He pesters me to death wanting me to tell him about what you did when we lived on Little Sam," Sarah told John.

"Fine looking young man you have there. And he sure is a talker for only being a little over two," John said to Sarah.

"Where is your husband, Bob?" John asked Sarah.

"He's dead," Sarah said.

"What happened to him?" John asked.

"I don't want to talk about it when my son is here. It's best he never knows about him," Sarah told John.

"If it's all right with you, I'll leave John with his Grandma and come back tomorrow and tell all about what has happened since I last saw you," Sarah told John.

The next morning John was at the place where his house was nearing the final stages of being finished. He looked toward the wagon road that led to the house and saw Sarah coming up the road through the trees. She was alone. John began walking to meet her near the trees. When they met, John said, "Let's sit over here under this big tree. We'll be out of the noise the workers are making."

"You asked me about my husband Bob. My son John never saw or knew him. I have never mentioned Bob to him."

"What happened to him?" John asked Sarah.

"I told you when you were here last that Bob was good to me. He never beat me or anything like that, but he was very jealous of me. He was furious when he found out that I was having a baby. He didn't come home to me anymore. He began to drink real heavy, and he slept in the store at night. Lots of days he never opened the store. Stayed in and drank any kind of whiskey he could get. His Daddy came down from New York to find out why the store was getting in debt. When he got here the store was locked. He opened and found Bob passed out drunk. When he woke up, his Dad told him he was closing the store until he thought Bob could run it again. He placed a closed sign in the window and returned to New York.

"Did he die in the store?" John asked.

"No," Sarah said.

She continued to tell how Bob died:

"As time went on, Bob drank more. He was getting his moonshine up the Pigeon River somewhere near Cold Mountain. Bob always had a car, and he was on his way up the river, and when he was going around a bad curve on a steep rock cliff around the narrow river road, the car ran off the road, and after it finished rolling, it went to rest in the river. Someone passing by saw the car and climbed down to where it was in the river. Bob was still in the car. The man that found Bob got some help, and they got him out and took him to the funeral home. The Sheriff was notified, and he came to my house and told me about him being dead.

"They called Bob's Dad in New York, and he came back to Canton. He had Bob put in a casket and sent back to his home up North. And that is how Bob died. I never knew him as a husband," Sarah said to John.

John didn't say anything. He stood up from where he had been sitting and said to Sarah, "Let's go have a look at the house."

"John, I have something I want you to hear before I leave," Sarah said to John.

"I'm sorry that I didn't believe that you would come back after the War and that I married Bob instead of waiting for you. I made a mistake. John, I still love you, and if you will forgive me I'm asking you if you will marry me. I promise I will make you a good wife, and we can spend many happy years together. Please forgive me," she said as tears ran down her cheeks.

John hung his head and didn't say anything for a few minutes. He then said, "Sarah, I loved you from the day you were fifteen years old. I waited all the many years I was away in the War, and when I returned and found that you were married, I was in shock. I guess I still love you, but I'll have to think it over before I give you an answer. I'll give you an answer tomorrow," John told Sarah.

"Come on. Let's go see the house," John said as he took Sarah by the hand.

After John went to his room at his Mom and Dad's house, he took the folder out and took out the letter Sergeant Davis had written him before he died.

"Don't make the mistake I made. .... There is always room for a second chance. .... Don't let happiness slip away. .... Forgive. ...."

John lay awake and he couldn't get the letter from Sergeant Davis out of his mind.

"Don't make the mistake I made ...." kept running through John's mind.

The next morning when Sarah came back to where the house was being built, she had little John with her. John met Sarah before she got to the house. He put his arms around her and said, "Sarah, I will marry you, and your son will be like he was my own. I want him to call me 'Daddy'."

As tears ran from both Sarah's and John's eyes, the little boy asked, "What's wrong, Mommy? Why are you and John crying?"

"We're not crying. We are happy," Sarah told him.

John and Sarah began to make plans for a wedding. They decided to wait until the house was complete and then have a small wedding at John's parents' house with John's and Sarah's families. They would have the preacher from the Baptist church over at Oak Grove marry them.

....

The house was finished, the wedding over. John, Sarah, and their young son, little John, were a family. The sun was setting, and the stars were beginning to come out. Sarah and John were sitting in their chairs on the porch of the new house. They could see all the lights at the paper mill and all over the town of Canton. In the far distance they could see the outline of many mountains — Shinning Rock, Cold Mountain, Devil's Court House, and many others they couldn't name.

"Time for you to get in bed," Sarah said to little John, who was curled up in his Dad's arms.

Sarah picked him up and headed to his room. John closed his eyes and said to himself, "My dreams have come true. I now have what I've dreamed of all these years— marrying Sarah Smith and living on Little Sam Mountain."

Afterword

Many years have passed since John returned from WW II and found that Sarah, his long-time sweetheart, was married. He left his home in Canton, North Carolina, and began traveling on a journey that took him half way around the world seeking happiness. After over two years, he returned from his journey to his place on Little Sam Mountain and built a house on the land he and Sarah had originally planned to build a house after he returned from World War II and got married.

John's good friend June Henson and Captain Moore were married and back in Kings Mountain where they had opened an office to practice medicine.

The girls that he met at the fish and chip shop were both married. Jane married her high school sweetheart after she had her baby from the American soldier who had promised to marry her before he disappeared.

Pam was still working as manager at the fish and chips restaurant and got married to David after he finished his military duty.

John's brother Joe was still working in the paper mill and his sister Betty was a nurse at the hospital in Waynesville.

John's Dad had retired from the paper mill . The family was still living on main street in Canton.

His best friend Sergeant Brad Davis was dead and had left his life's savings to John.

Many things had happened since he returned from his journey

John and Sarah found happiness after they were married after the tragic death of Sarah's husband. After their marriage, the family increased. Another boy and two girls were born.

The children went off to school. John was a retired businessman. He had purchased the store from Bob's father and leased it to a long-time employee of the store.

This book, *Little Sam Mountain — The Journey*, written and published after I became ninety years old, is my sixth book. I was eighty-four when I wrote my first book. All of my books are written from memories of my life in the mountains of Western North Carolina.

****

Other books by
Charles C. Fletcher:

Out West and Back

The Panther on Cold Mountain and Other Stories

Little Sam Mountain

The Sheriff

Grassy Top Mountain